THE SHADOW OF DAPH

WEDDINGS. FUNERALS. SLEUTHING.

PHILLIPA NEFRI CLARK

The Shadow of Daph

Copyright © 2021 Phillipa Nefri Clark

All rights reserved. By payment of the required fees, you have been granted the non-exclusive, non-transferable right to access and read the text of this e-book on-screen. No part of this text may be reproduced, transmitted, down-loaded, decompiled, reverse engineered, or stored in or introduced into any information storage and retrieval system, in any form or by any means, whether electronic or mechanical, now known or hereinafter invented, without the express written permission of the publisher and the author.

All characters in this book have no existence outside the imagination of the author and have no relation whatsoever to anyone bearing the same name or names. They are not even distantly inspired by any individual known or unknown to the author, and all incidents are pure invention.

Paperback ISBN: 978-0-6453095-0-8
Hardcover ISBN: 978-0-6453095-2-2

Cover design by Steam Power Studios
Editing by NasDean.com

A QUICK NOTE...

This series is set in Australia and written in Aussie/British English for an authentic experience.

CHANGE OF PLANS

"Daph, you'll need to check the map again. I'm worried I'll miss the turn off with so little light. We just passed Conways Track." John Jones didn't take his eyes off the narrow road.

Daphne Jones grabbed the map which had fallen into the footwell near her handbag. "Got it. Conways Track? Hm." She traced the route with her finger which John had highlighted in red at their last stop. Then she turned it upside down. "Okie dokie. Another three curves, no, two seeing as you've done one. Another two curves and then there's a bridge. Just after that you need to take a left."

"Is there a street name?"

"Shady Bend Road."

John laughed shortly. "Plenty of shade here." He slowed to navigate another long curve and Daphne glanced in the side mirror at Bluebell. Their beautiful caravan made their travels a little more challenging at times but was a blessing they would never leave behind. Turning the car and caravan around on such a narrow road was not something John would want to try if they missed their turnoff. And not so close to nightfall. Daphne leaned forward to better see the road ahead.

"Kangaroo at two o'clock!"

John touched the brakes as the headlights reflected in the eyes of a grey kangaroo staring at them from the side of the road. "Stay there, Mister Roo." A joey popped its head out of an oversized pouch. "Whoops, sorry. Missus Roo."

When they'd left their last stop a few hours ago, they'd planned on already being settled into a new town, where Daphne would officiate a wonderful wedding on the weekend. But then her phone had rung and within minutes they were on a different road.

"Daph, you said a bridge then a right turn?"

"Left, John. I wish there were some lights along here. One might break down and never be found."

John really needed to put one of those digital location things in the car. A GPS. Maps made little sense to Daphne and she navigated under duress.

"I think that's it!" she pointed ahead. "Over the bridge and almost straight away there's a sign."

A moment later they'd turned onto Shady Bend Road, which curved up a steep hill. Bluebell weighed them down and John changed to a lower gear. According to the car clock it was a little after six, which in late spring was still daylight. It was the heavy canopy of gum, wattle, and blackwood trees towering over the road which made visibility so poor.

"We'll pull in somewhere in the town to find out where we can stop tonight." John said.

"I've got the name of the place but not an address. Shall I check the message?"

"Think we're almost there." Even as he spoke, they reached the crest of the hill and the trees gave way to houses. Bigger properties at first, then smaller and closer together as they approached a township. The speed limit dropped and houses changed to a row of shops on either side of the road. Unlike the roads they'd left behind, there was hardly a tree in sight. For that matter, hardly a car or a person either.

"Guess it is after closing time for most shops. Is that parking space big enough for us?"

John nosed the car alongside the pavement about halfway through the town. "Good spotting, doll."

"Doesn't look like much is going on here." She checked her phone for the message which had arrived after the phone call. "Shady Bend Camping Ground. Can't be too hard to find?"

"How about we duck into the supermarket over the road? We can get directions and pick up the shopping you wanted." He climbed out and met Daphne on the footpath. After locking the car, he held his arm out. "Be good to get to our camping site before night completely falls."

Daphne tucked her arm through his. "I'll zoom around the supermarket while you get directions. Only need a couple of things for dinner so it won't take long at all."

It was just as well both she and John were flexible with arrangements.

There was no room at the suggested camping ground thanks to a local event which had drawn competitors from around the state. They were directed to an unpowered ground in the next town. At least it was only a few minutes' drive away and the lack of power would be manageable for one or two nights. As John performed his ritual of checking Bluebell was secure and had no ill effects from what had been a relatively short drive, Daphne read the message again.

Dear Daphne, following our phone call I want to thank you

profusely for changing your plans to accommodate our late notice request.

The phone call from Fred Yates had surprised Daphne.

The deceased is a local resident of some note and her passing leaves many of our community saddened. On consultation with her daughter, a decision was made to reach out to someone with a proven record of great compassion. Your name was put forward.

Who had recommended her services?

The funeral tomorrow has every arrangement made, but the deceased's daughter asked me to find a suitable person to help say goodbye to our beloved Edwina and celebrate her memory. Attached is information about her life, her place in the community and achievements, along with certain requests.

She'd look at those once they settled in and had the generator going. Easier to view on the laptop.

"Think we're right. Not much point using the awning tonight." John unlocked Bluebell. "Sorry, thought I'd done this."

"Oh, I could have used my key but I was keen to take another look at the message from Mr Yates."

"If I turn on the lamps, are you happy to do a quick check in here while I get the generator going?"

"Can you pass me the shopping first?"

It took little time to unpack the shopping and turn on the lamps which were a clever addition when Bluebell was refurbished. An addition to the usual lighting, these lamps were solar powered from panels on the roof of the caravan. Perfect for using at times like this and meant once the generator was off, they'd still have light.

John kicked the generator into action and then joined her with a smile.

"Not ideal but we're getting better at making do."

She glanced at her watch. "I should get the pasta started."

"What if I do dinner?" John gave her a big hug. "You, my celebrant sleuth, have to prepare for tomorrow."

Daphne grinned. John's funny term always made her smile. "As long as you don't mind. But I'm not here for sleuthing." She squeezed him back and wiggled out of his arms. "I shall find my notebook and get started."

Halfway to the bedroom, she glanced back. "John? Thanks for this. For agreeing without hesitation to come here on a moment's notice."

"Anytime. It is a small detour and will give me an unexpected chance to visit another graveyard. Assuming you don't mind me being there at the same time, albeit in another part?"

John's passion for genealogy fitted well with Daphne's new career. He visited the local graveyards and small churches to work on a project he said little about. But it made him happy and Daphne loved seeing him enjoy doing something for himself.

"You are most welcome. Always."

Notebook and pen in hand, Daphne settled at the table. John set a pot of water on the gas cooktop alongside a deep pan. He chopped lots of tomatoes, onions, mushrooms, and a selection of herbs. As the aromas drifted across, Daphne's tummy rumbled in response. She enjoyed John's cooking and now they were on the road most of the time, he more than shared the load. The only thing he couldn't outdo were her homemade cookies.

She scribbled a shopping list on a spare piece of paper. Flour. Choc chips. Extra butter. Tomorrow would be a busy one but there was always time to do a bit of baking.

After opening the laptop, Daphne located an email from Fred with the extra information and printed the couple of pages out. The little printer was so useful and took up barely any space in one of the cupboards. At the top of the page, she wrote out the timetable for the next day.

10am. Meet with Mr Yates and concerned parties to go over the ceremony. (Allow one hour)

1pm. Quick lunch and get ready.

2pm. Funeral.

In between the meeting and lunch, she'd finalise her words. She had a lot of ideas bubbling in her head based on what she'd read so far and would write them first thing in the morning. Her mind was at its sharpest early in the day. She'd not officiated many funerals but she would make Edwina's send-off special. A memorable day for her family and friends.

Over dinner, Daphne filled John in on more of the details. He wasn't disappointed by the sudden change of destination as this region was on his 'to visit' list anyway. The list he kept on his phone.

"Edwina Drinkwater passed away at her home from natural causes. She's only sixty though, so it seems a bit young for natural causes. Anyway, she has one relative, a daughter. Sonia." Daphne read from the notes she'd handwritten on the printed pages.

"Some more mineral water?" John collected the bottle from the fridge. "Nice with the lime, isn't it?"

"Very. And this pasta is as good as any from a restaurant, love."

Daphne was always the first to compliment a person. Her kind heart and generous soul drew him to her in their last year of high school, and if anything, her love of people was even more obvious with this late life change of career.

"She lived alone, although her daughter has her own

cottage on the same property. She had a busy life. Owns a small shop. Oh, this is interesting. She sold the wares of local craftspeople, artists, and amateur cooks. Preserves, jams, cakes…there's a list. And she was president of the Rural Craft, Cooking, and Creation Society. RCCCS. Sounds a bit like the Country Women's Association." Daphne rolled linguine around her fork. "I imagine she'll be missed."

"What else do you know about tomorrow?"

"Mm…this was so nice." Daphne said. "Edwina lived in Shady Bend most of her life. She was divorced but there is no mention about her ex-husband. Sounds like a normal life in a normal town. And she donated to a local wildlife sanctuary."

"I'm sure you will find some beautiful words to comfort her loved ones, Daph. It must make it so much easier when you're officiating for someone who was a nice person."

"Yes. Yes, I think Edwina Drinkwater was a nice woman who will be deeply missed."

NOT MISSED AT ALL

"She was a horrible person and I'm glad she's dead!"

Those were the last words Daphne had expected from the daughter of the deceased, let alone spat with a venom completely at odds with the woman's appearance.

Silence cut through the room like the proverbial knife as all eyes turned in various levels of shock to Sonia Drinkwater. She folded her arms and lifted her chin, defying anyone to disagree. A slender woman with oversized glasses and long straight hair, she gave off a sweet girl-from-the-country vibe. Until she opened her mouth.

Daphne had arrived at the funeral home on time, soft briefcase in hand with her notebook and draft speech ready for approval or adjustments. Shady Bend Funeral Home was set in pretty gardens surrounded by gum trees, with a circular driveway and a central lawn, not far from the middle of the town. Fred Yates was outside the front door with a woman he'd introduced as Tracy Chappell. He was in his early sixties while she was a decade younger, by Daphne's estimation. In a sombre suit, Fred was solemn, balding, and double-chinned. Tracy wore jeans and a T-shirt proclaiming

'Judge and Juror' with a picture on its front of a cake being hit with a gavel.

Fred ushered them inside.

Through double doors was a small entry area with an unattended desk and a bell. Hallways went off in several directions but Fred led them through another set of double doors to a large but quiet reception room with soft lighting and sofas. Sonia, perhaps thirty years old, was already there. She sat cross-legged and didn't get up, but removed her glasses to stare at Daphne.

Ten minutes into the meeting, Daphne asked if there was anything special to highlight about Edwina and the resulting explosion of fury and bitterness ensued. In the sincere hope she wasn't making things worse, Daphne got to her feet and joined Sonia.

"I'm so sorry, dear."

Sonia blinked at Daphne and then a single tear trickled down her cheek. Fred moved fast to provide a box of tissues and Daphne took it with a smile, holding them close to Sonia.

"What would *you* like to happen at the funeral?" Daphne kept her voice soft. "How do you want to say goodbye?"

In the few months of Daphne's new celebrant life, she'd officiated at a handful of funerals, plus a few goodbye ceremonies. Actually, two of the latter and both in a town they'd left only a couple of weeks ago. And that was a whole other story. Although her practical experience might be limited, she had a lifetime of being a people person. Always the shoulder to cry on for friends and acquaintances. The person who would listen and then gently offer kind words. It worked most of the time.

"I'd like…I think that…" Sonia's tone hardened. "I want to see her dropped into that hole and covered up as fast as possible. There's already been far too much money spent on an elaborate casket let alone flowers and all the other costs." She leaned back and crossed her arms as well. "That sounds like the best way to say goodbye. See the back of her."

"Enough, Sonia, give it a rest." This was Tracy. "You'll still get a nice little windfall. Not like anyone will throw you off the property."

The two women glared at each other and Daphne retreated to her previous seat. Whatever history there was should be shelved until after the funeral. She glanced at her notes. There was nothing in them to indicate anything other than a community filled with love and respect for the deceased.

Fred poured water into four glasses from a jug on a stand near the door. "Who would care for some water?"

Daphne nodded and he brought one across.

"Only if there's something…extra in it." Sonia announced.

Tracy rolled her eyes as she got to her feet. "Thanks, Fred." She took a glass from him. "Mrs Jones, I'd like to speak at the funeral. I've known Edwina for decades and we've worked together on committees for longer than I care to admit. So how do we make this happen?"

"Once Sonia approves the ceremony, I'll then add anyone who wishes to speak in order and will introduce them. Do you know of any others?"

Fred sat opposite. "Only two others apart from Tracy. The first is Desmond. Desmond Rogers. He considered Edwina to be a close friend and—"

"Get real." Sonia reached for a handbag and stood. "Nobody liked her so it is all lip service."

"Ilona adored her." Fred said, getting to his own feet. "And Ilona is the other person who wishes to speak. Why not put aside your feelings until after the funeral, Sonia? In a few hours this will all be a memory. Rather than rake up old upsets, shouldn't we all try to get along for this short time and do the right thing?"

Sonia, who had seemed intent on stalking out of the room, came to a halt near Fred. Instead to doing what Daphne had half-expected and continuing with her snipy comments, the younger woman dropped her head and nodded.

"This is a dreadful time, Sonia. Stressful and distressing. But if you can be the bigger person in all of this, you'll respect yourself later on. And if I can do this, so can you."

All of this was quite interesting. It was one thing for a funeral director to offer support and comfort but quite another to counsel a grieving client on how to behave. And what had he meant by if *he* could do this? Sonia returned to her seat. Tracy, meanwhile, was tapping on her phone.

"You mentioned a person called Ilona?" It was time to take control back. "What do I need to know about her so I can ensure she has the appropriate time to speak?"

All three looked at her as if she was supposed to already know.

She didn't.

"Ilona is, was, my mother's closest friend. Probably only real friend." Sonia said. "And she is a wedding celebrant. Like you. Except she is," Sonia gestured quote marks with her fingers, "Too shattered to officiate. So, if she wouldn't pull her head out to look after her best friend's funeral, I had to ask Fred to find someone else."

Do you ever say anything nice about anyone?

"I believe Mrs Drinkwater had a special request." Daphne summoned a smile. "In the notes I received—and I have to thank you, Fred, for such comprehensive information—Mrs Drinkwater wished to bestow gifts on every person who attended the funeral as a reminder of her affection for them."

Something like a choke emanated from Sonia, which Daphne chose to ignore.

"I understand there will be a table set up after the funeral which will include a selection of items from the shop she owned. I think it is a lovely gesture."

It was interesting how each of the other people in the room responded.

Fred nodded the whole time she spoke.

Sonia shook her head.

Tracy put down her phone and ran her tongue over her lips. Her eyes were elsewhere—somewhere faraway. Was she imagining some delicious fare from the shop?

Someone's phone rang and the moment was gone. Fred apologised and hurried from the room, reaching into a pocket. Tracy had a small smile on her face but was back in the present. "I didn't know Edwina had made last wishes. Rather nice of the old girl."

"Old girl. Really? You are almost the same age." Sonia snapped.

Tracy burst out laughing.

Before things got out of hand, Daphne located the draft ceremony. "Sonia, would you mind taking a look? If there are any changes, I can make them now."

"It doesn't matter. Say whatever you wish."

"I'd feel more comfortable knowing you were satisfied with my wording. If you don't mind?"

With a sigh, Sonia took the couple of sheets of paper and read. At least the room was quiet while she did, apart from the low tapping sound as Tracy's focus returned to her phone. Daphne snuck a look at her own but the signal was too low to even send a message. With luck it was better outside, otherwise she had a long wait ahead. John had dropped her there and was going to see if there was a powered camping site anywhere else to move Bluebell.

Which led her to a question.

"Excuse me, what is the event on in town? We tried to find a powered site for our caravan last night and had to go to the next town."

"Oh, that's just our local agricultural show." Tracy answered without looking up. "The livestock exhibitors always pile in early to settle their horses and whatnot. Today we begin preliminary judging of the crafts, baking, bottling and so on. Get things ready for the finals."

Was Tracy a judge? Her T-shirt made sense if she was. Daphne hadn't been to a country show in years. Not since… well since her childhood. Animals. Rides with carnival music. Laughter. Sticky sweet treats. People everywhere. Her father yelling. Furious with her.

Daphne's heart thudded.

"So sorry to disappear like that. Had to take the call." Fred returned.

The music subsided. Not that anyone else heard it. She released a breath she'd not meant to hold. Had anyone noticed her hands shake?

"Shall we finalise the details?" Fred asked. "I think your husband is parked outside, Mrs Jones."

Not only was John parked along the grass verge, but a motor scooter was behind him. Daphne was partway along the path to the road when the rider alighted and removed their helmet. A woman.

John stepped out of the car.

"Hello-o. Are you Daphne?" The woman flapped both her arms as though to get Daphne's attention. "I really need to speak with you."

The woman was in her mid-forties, dressed in an ankle

length black dress and wearing fresh flowers in bright red hair that flowed to her waist.

"I am Daphne."

"Oh, I thought so! My cousin described you and you are exactly as he said."

Cousin?

"Um…how did he describe me?"

Sure you should ask, Daph?

The other woman smiled, softening her expression. She wasn't pretty as such but had a kindness in her eyes which warmed Daphne to her.

"He said you had cute streaks of colour in your hair, wore fashionable glasses, and know how to carry off a nice suit. He also said you have a beautiful smile." The woman held her hand out. "I'm Ilona."

They shook hands. John rested his arms on the roof of the car.

"I'm so sorry for your loss, Ilona. I understand Mrs Drinkwater was your friend."

"Yes. Edie meant the world to me and I miss her so much." Ilona blinked a few times. Close up, the rims of her eyes were red. "I really can't believe she's gone."

"What can I do to help you? I believe you have asked to speak this afternoon?"

Ilona nodded. "If I don't speak for Edie, nobody will. Oh, I know Sonia and Tracy and perhaps Desmond will stand up but I'm the one who knew her. Do you know what I mean? I was her confidante and understood her."

"Then you must speak. I didn't know her, but with such a close friend I would imagine she'd treasure having your unique words heard. Is there anything in particular you'd like me to know first. Anything I can include in my ceremony to help."

All of a sudden, Ilona threw her arms around Daphne in a hug. "This is why you are here, dear Daphne."

The hug was quick and Ilona stepped back with a hint of embarrassment on her face. "I don't do funerals. Never could. Weddings, naming ceremonies. All the good, happy stuff is fine, but I'm too big a sook to manage to help people say goodbye. But I heard you are wonderful with sad times."

Not sure I'd like that on my website!

"Ilona, who is your cousin?"

"I am so sorry? I thought you knew. Maurice. He met you in Little Bridges."

Her shoulders dropped. As much as she liked Maurice, who owned the local newspaper in Little Bridges, hearing the name of the town was an unwanted reminder of how quickly things can go wrong.

TOO MUCH TO BEAR

"Is that town going to follow us around forever?" Daphne grumbled as she applied makeup in the small bathroom in their caravan. Lunch had been little more than a quick sandwich and there was no time for even one cup of tea. A call from Fred had requested she be at the funeral home earlier than first planned.

"Little Bridges?" John leaned against a cupboard outside the bathroom. "I wouldn't let it upset you. Even though it was stressful, just think of how you helped find a killer. Something to be proud of."

Not long ago, Daphne was the celebrant at a country wedding which went horribly wrong. Against her better judgement she'd become involved in working out who was behind some dreadful crimes. And it was satisfying but hardly the kind of thing she wanted on her calling card!

"I suppose something good came of it. And Maurice was kind to recommend me. We could leave after the funeral if you prefer." Daphne chose a lipstick to match the top she wore. It might seem a bit much for a funeral, but another of Edwina's requests was that every attendee wore at least one bright colour. Thank goodness Daphne had a lovely hot pink blouse which fit the bill and worked well under the elegant black jacket she'd don at the last minute.

"Wouldn't mind taking some photos this afternoon. There's a gorge not far away with a waterfall. Might get something good enough to print out and frame for the house."

Since retiring as owner and principal realtor of Rivers End Real Estate, John had turned his mind to new activities. Genealogy of course, but also photography plus a renewed interest in river fishing. There were few things which filled her heart more than seeing her husband of forty plus years enjoying their nomadic life.

"If you don't mind, I'll come with you. A waterfall sounds like a perfect place to relax after a sad funeral."

Make up done, Daphne was ready. Jacket, handbag, and briefcase with her embossed ceremony book were all she needed. There were mourners who deserved to help say goodbye and she wasn't about to keep them waiting.

The reception room where Daphne met earlier with Fred, Sonia, and Tracy, was transformed with the comfortable seating pushed back to make space for a long trestle table with smaller tables and plastic chairs dotted around.

On the table was a tower of small plates and plastic glasses, along with napkins and plastic cutlery. Laid out at both ends were plates of scones, slices, cupcakes, and other baked goods, while the middle had been raised with boxes to form a second level. This overflowed with sealed bottles of preserves, jams, fruit, chutneys, sauces, framed artwork, and small gift-wrapped boxes. There was barely room for another plate, yet at the far end a woman managed to wiggle one more in.

"Think we might leave the rest in the kitchen." The woman smiled at Daphne. "Hello, I'm Petra West."

"Nice to meet you, Petra. I'm Daphne, the celebrant."

"Very good of you to come on such short notice. We are all most appreciative." Petra wandered around the table checking everything. "This is for after…well, once poor Edwina is…well, you know."

"It looks delicious. Is all of this locally made?"

"Oh yes. Our little community loves local and Edwina was passionate about us all creating perfect products for the customers. You should try some of the rhubarb and apricot jam on a scone. I had a taste in the kitchen and it is something to behold."

Not a fan of rhubarb, or sampling the wares meant for a wake, Daphne was about to politely refuse when Fred arrived, followed by a younger man dressed in a similar suit.

"Mrs Jones, hello and thank you. I wanted you to meet the pall bearers before we left. The funeral home is providing three of them, including Zeke here. The others are friends of the deceased who volunteered. Zeke, this is Mrs Jones, who will officiate the ceremony."

Daphne and Zeke shook hands but his eyes were on the table.

Fred continued. "I see you've already met Petra. And you spoke with Tracy earlier. Our remaining person is Desmond Rogers who—ah, there you are."

"Apologies. The old car didn't want to start again so it was a case of walk here instead." Desmond Rogers was in his seventies. Not a tall man, his black jacket barely covered a large stomach which wobbled as he shuffled across the floor with a slight limp. Daphne couldn't help comparing his face to that of a bulldog.

"Desmond, this is Mrs Jones, who changed her itinerary to help us out. Desmond is…was, Edwina's neighbour."

Daphne shook Desmond's hand. "My condolences."

"Yes. Sad state of affairs. Heart attack. Expected, but not so soon. Never so soon."

Tracy emerged from another room carrying a tray of filled champagne glasses. "Everyone! Time to make a toast. I have no idea where Sonia is but we haven't got time to wait around for her."

She placed the tray on a table and took a moment to hand out each glass. "Fred. Desmond. Zeke, you're driving so not for you. Ah, Petra, here's yours."

Daphne retreated close to the door, not wanting to intrude on this moment. Once everybody else had a glass, Tracy proposed a toast.

"To living life the way you want. To being the person you enjoy being. To Edwina."

There was a murmur of agreement, some clinks of glasses, and then silence as champagne was sipped.

"Be the person you enjoy being, even when it makes everyone else hate you."

Daphne glanced around. The words were softly spoken by a person in the hallway. A woman about her own age, shorter than Daphne and with short cropped brown hair. Her arms were wrapped around her body and she gazed into the room at the group.

"Hello, dear. Would you care to come in?" Daphne made herself known.

If the other woman was concerned her words had been overheard, she said nothing, but stepped inside and looked at Daphne with interest.

"I like your hair." She announced.

"Well, thank you."

Tracy drifted over with more glasses on the tray. "Mrs Jones, please have some. Hello, Amanda."

"I'm fine, thank you for offering." Daphne said. "Best keep my mind focused on the important time ahead."

"Fair enough." Tracy turned to leave.

"But I'd like one." Amanda reached out for a glass.

Tracy held the tray out of reach and kept walking. Amanda followed, grabbing at the tray. With a crash, it hit the ground, glasses shattering and golden liquid bubbling on the carpet.

"Look what you did!" Tracy hissed at Amanda. "I was trying to avoid disaster but no, you always find a way to mess things up. This special time here is just for the pall bearers of which you are not one."

Petra rushed over with a roll of paper towels and small bin and began carefully collecting pieces of glass. Zeke squatted to help, immediately cutting himself.

"Take more care, Zeke! You'll get blood on the carpet." Tracy scooped up the tray and stalked to the kitchen.

"Don't mind her, hon." Petra wrapped his thumb with a sheet of paper towel and shooed him away with a smile.

Amanda watched on with no outward response. Desmond and Fred kept out of it.

Good thinking. Tensions were running high and in Daphne's experience, stress often showed a side of people they usually hid away. Well, she was learning a lot about the personalities in this room. And the oddest part was how little they actually liked each other, which was not the face they'd all tried to portray. What an interesting funeral this would be.

John wandered into the Shady Bend Cemetery a few minutes before Daphne's start time. His purpose was quite different to hers and he had his phone and a notebook ready to record anything of interest. The cemetery wasn't large and he had no desire to intrude on the funeral so kept his distance up a small hill, but even so, he was unable to avoid seeing the funeral party.

Daphne was graveside, along with a growing group of mourners. All wore black but each had a dash of colour. The woman who rode the motor scooter earlier was still in her long black dress but now had a sash of woven flowers around her waist. Others were less flamboyant. A yellow tie here, a blue set of shoes there. Daphne noticed him and waved discreetly.

After waving back, John turned his attention to the headstones. Here, in this tiny forest town, was there a clue to finding someone from Daphne's life? A father she'd probably never met. It was his secret mission and every little town was an opportunity to search. He took his notebook out and read through some of his scribbles from another graveyard.

There was a noise. A cry followed by a dull thud. And screams. His heart jolted. Something terrible was happening at the funeral.

How comforting John's presence was. Funerals were quite new. She'd attended too many in her lifetime and officiated a few, but it was hard work to separate her emotions from the motions. The sorrow and grief around her were profound and as more people arrived, many openly weeping, her heart cried. Seeing her beloved husband at a distance helped. He always gave her strength.

One of Fred's staff had given her a lift over and they'd

arrived before the hearse so she was able to spend a few minutes gathering herself and setting up a little spot for the speakers to stand. The grave was a couple of rows from the carpark, overlooked by beautiful flowering trees. A peaceful place to rest.

Ilona arrived soon after and although she'd offered a sad smile, said nothing as she found a place near the foot of the grave, her eyes glistening.

Within a few minutes there was a crowd. This funeral had no seating, but there was a small table which held a hundred or so yellow roses. Each mourner collected one on their way.

Sonia stalked from the carpark. She wore black with no sign of colour and ignored the roses. She walked right around the grave and chose a spot halfway between Daphne and Ilona.

Fred joined Daphne. "They are on their way. It'll take a little while with Desmond's wonky knee, but he insisted. Better slow than sorry."

Her ceremony book open, Daphne cast an eye over the words. She was here for these sad folk. Here to lay their dear one to rest. It was a time of loss and mourning but also of celebration of a life well lived. A life which had made a difference.

The casket approached. Desmond and Petra at the front. Two of the staff in the middle. Zeke and Tracy at the back with Tracy counting their steps aloud. Left. And right. Left. And right.

Daphne couldn't recall ever seeing someone at the back direct the pallbearers. But Tracy did give the impression of needing to take charge even if she wasn't doing a good job of keeping everyone in step.

The casket wobbled.

Something's wrong.

Petra wasn't in time. Not even close. As they crossed the

short grass between graves she faltered, forcing the others to adjust their grips. Tracy didn't look impressed.

"Lift a bit higher, Pet. We're almost there for goodness sake."

They reached the side of grave and a silence fell. There was no birdsong. No breeze in the trees. No whispers from the crowd.

Petra swayed and then leaned against the casket which visibly shook.

"Petra. Stand up." Tracy whispered loudly.

"My stomach. Help...me…"

Petra's skin was red and glistening with sweat. Her eyes rolled into the top of her skull. Releasing the handle, she thudded onto the ground.

Mourners cried out.

The other pallbearers tried to compensate but Desmond overbalanced and let go of his handle, almost falling as well.

The casket dropped with a dull thump onto its side.

There was a collective gasp.

All eyes were on the casket.

On the latch of the lid somehow undone.

On a narrow gap which shouldn't be there.

Everybody stepped back except for Fred, who dropped to his knees beside the lid. From a pocket he drew out car keys, rummaging through them to find a tiny flashlight. He blinked a couple of times as if to gather his courage, and then pointed the light into the gap.

Zeke joined him, squatting to peer into the casket.

"Leave it, Zeke." Fred's elbow shot out as if to force the younger man away. "We'll right it and seal it again."

"But sir…"

"I said leave it alone. Help the others."

"But, how?" Zeke straightened and gazed at Daphne through startled eyes. "It's empty."

A CATASTROPHE

The scene was chaotic.

Petra lay groaning on the grass, clutching her stomach after regaining consciousness.

Desmond was down as well, but sitting upright as Tracy checked his ankle.

Zeke and Fred covered the casket—or at least what they could—with their suit jackets and those from the other funeral home employees.

People were all over the place. Some on their phones, even taking photographs. Others holding on to each other in shock.

"Someone call an ambulance!" Daphne looked for John. He was jogging towards her with his phone out, tapping as he went.

Ilona hadn't moved from the end of the grave. Her face was ashen and her lips mouthed something Daphne couldn't work out. Perhaps it was 'Edie'. Hopefully, she would keep an eye on how close she was to the edge and not take the wrong step.

And Sonia? She was laughing. Tears poured down her face as chortles racked her body.

Amidst the pandemonium, nobody was caring for Petra. Daphne stepped around the casket and lowered herself onto the grass.

"Petra? Can you hear me, dear?"

Petra turned wide, frightened eyes to Daphne, opening and closing her mouth with no words. Her eyelids fluttered and she was unconscious.

Daphne undid the buttons on her jacket and slipped it off to gently cover Petra. The woman was breathing but her skin was hot and clammy. This wasn't fainting. Daphne searched the faces around her, all intent on their own worries. Amanda appeared through the crowd.

"Can you help? Do you know if Petra has any underlying conditions?" Daphne asked.

For a moment Amanda stood there without a word, her eyes darting around, but then she kneeled beside them both. Her hand went to Petra's neck, fingers against her pulse, and she counted against her own watch. John was there, behind her, talking on his phone.

Amanda leaned back. "She needs to get to hospital. And I mean a big hospital with an intensive care unit. We need a rescue helicopter."

John put his phone away and leaned down. "Ambulance is coming."

"Won't be enough." Amanda brushed a strand of hair from Petra's face. "Can you find some blankets. Or a priest."

"A priest?"

"Doubt she'll make it to the hospital. Poor love."

John helped Daphne to her feet. "I have a blanket in the car. Back in a minute."

Amanda began singing to Petra. It was a childhood lullaby

Daphne knew but didn't quite remember and a shiver went down her spine. It was bizarre. Amanda rocking in time with the song as she held Petra's hand. Petra lay in a pool of sunlight and Daphne moved to cast a shadow across her. The poor woman didn't need the heat of the day directly on her face.

"Mrs Jones!"

Fred gestured from the other side of the casket.

"Amanda, can you stay with Petra? Please give her some shade." Daphne touched the other woman's shoulder and received a nod in response. "Be right back."

Her handbag and briefcase were still at the head of the grave and she collected them before joining Fred, who had Zeke and his two other staff with him. His tie was crooked and he'd rolled his shirt sleeves up. He glanced at Daphne then turned to Zeke.

"Would you three ensure nobody gets photos or video of this? Just be polite and discreet but we need to protect the deceased's privacy."

The three men fanned out and Fred took a deep breath, closing his eyes for a moment.

"Fred, what a dreadful shock for you all. There's an ambulance on its way."

His eyes opened. "Ambulance? Bit late for that."

"For Petra. She's not in a good way. And I imagine Desmond might need his ankle looked at."

For that matter, Sonia could use someone to check she was alright.

The laughter had subsided to an occasional cackle. Sonia sat cross-legged at the side of the grave, occasionally tossing a blade of grass or piece of dirt in.

"Oh dear. I thought Petra fainted. What is wrong with her? We can't have another scandal here and as for Sonia…" his shoulders slumped. "This will be the final straw for her."

"Another scandal?"

"There's always something. You said an ambulance is coming. What about the police?" He called to Zeke. "Give the police station a ring, mate."

Always some scandal? Daphne had a familiar sensation in her gut. Last time she felt this, she'd soon found herself knee-deep in a murder mystery. Her senses tingled.

"What did you do with her?" An angry, tear-filled voice screamed. Ilona was on the move. Other mourners stepped aside as she powered her way to the casket.

Fred got in between it and Ilona and held his hand up. "Please, please, Ilona, I know you are upset. We are all upset—"

"Upset? Upset?" Ilona stopped short of Fred. The flowers around her waist were gone, leaving her long dress ballooning about her. "Where is she?" She tried to push past Fred to go to the casket and he grabbed onto her arms.

"You can't go there. I promise we'll find out where she is. I promise you."

"This is…this is your fault." With a sob, Ilona wrenched herself away and ran in the opposite direction, long hair whipping behind her.

"Should someone go after her?" Daphne asked. She took a step or two in the same direction but Ilona was a fast runner and was already almost out of sight between trees. "Someone needs to check on her."

Fred's eyes were on Sonia. "She's laughing."

"Shock does odd things to people."

"For goodness sake, Fred, of course she'd find this funny." Tracy stood on the other side of the casket. "Just ignore her and she'll sort herself out. In the meantime, Desmond needs to see a doctor for his ankle and we really need to get Amanda away from poor Petra." She rolled her eyes. "Why don't you go and find out what you did with Edwina and I'll shoo everyone out of the cemetery."

"I didn't do anything with Edwina." Fred spun around, his face turning even redder. "She was in…well, in there. At least she was last night and everything was done properly. How on earth could this happen to me?" He pulled at the knot of his tie to loosen it and undid the top button. "And no. It isn't up to you to send mourners home. The police will be here and they can decide if the ceremony can continue."

Without the deceased?

Daphne could just see it. The casket would be turned onto its base. The people regathered. And she would resume her place and begin the ceremony. Well, that might work if nobody knew the casket was empty. But they did. And Sonia would laugh hysterically while Ilona cried and Tracy bossed everyone around.

"Daph? I've put the blanket over the lady but she's been left alone. The minute we could hear the siren, the other lady jumped up and dashed away."

"Why would Amanda leave her?" Daphne followed John and so did Tracy and Fred. Petra was barely breathing.

"Amanda knows she shouldn't have even touched her." Tracy kneeled down. "I had no idea she was like this. Sorry, Pet. Help is coming. Where's her handbag? She'll need her phone and stuff in hospital."

"In the hearse. Unless she left them at the funeral home. I'll check." Fred was gone before anyone could reply.

"I don't understand." Daphne said. "Why shouldn't Amanda have sat with her? She took her pulse so looked as though she has some training."

Tracy laughed shortly. "She does. Used to be the town doctor." She made the motion of someone drinking. "Bit too much of this. Lost her licence. But I reckon our Petra's been poisoned and it wouldn't surprise me one bit if Amanda Sinclair is responsible."

John made two more trips to the car. One to take the blanket back when the paramedics took over, and then to find some water for Daphne. She'd left her bottle in the footwell rather than take it to the ceremony and now, instead of being ready to go home, she had no idea when she could leave.

Once again they were at the scene of a crime…or at the very least, the scene of several awful mishaps.

After putting the water bottle into Daphne's hand and seeing her take a few sips, he excused himself. He'd dropped his notebook up near the trees when the commotion began. It took a few minutes but he spied it on the grass, sprawled open.

He scooped it up. Nearby, a muffled sob alerted him to someone partly hidden behind one of the trees. And she was crying. His heart went out to her. She leaned against the trunk of a tree with her head in her hands and her legs drawn up against her body. It was the woman who'd spoken to Daphne near the car this morning.

John made sure he stepped on a couple of twigs as he approached, so as not to startle her. She glanced up and wiped her eyes.

"I'm John. Daphne's husband. It's Ilona, isn't it? Would you like me to get you some water?"

"Um…no. But you are kind to offer. I'm overwhelmed. I just don't know what to think."

"Understandable. Such a shock."

She nodded. The tears stopped and she took a couple of short, sharp breaths, then stood. Her hand went into a pocket in her dress and she pulled out a tissue. "Nobody else understood Edie like me. People think she was harsh in her judgement of them and perhaps she was, but there was always a reason why. And now they'll all fight it out to get her secret recipe." She blew her nose. "I'm not good with confrontation but if anyone is mean about her, I will say something."

"I would hope nobody would take advantage of the situation to be unkind, but if they do, that is a reflection on them. Not on Edie." John said. "Hopefully, this is all a simple mix up. Possibly the wrong casket was collected. Would you like to go back down there and see if there is any news?"

Her eyes drifted to the grave and John followed her line of sight. People were trailing out of the cemetery. The few who remained were close to the casket. The poor woman the paramedics had just loaded onto their ambulance—handbag tucked under her blanket—had looked gravely ill to John. Not at all responsive to their care and there was talk of meeting a helicopter to transport her to the closest hospital equipped to assist her. Nobody seemed to have an idea what was wrong but he'd overheard the comment from the louder woman. The one about poison.

With every fibre of his being, he wanted it to be untrue.

Daphne gazed up towards them and John raised his hand and waved.

"You should go to her. Your wife has been so lovely and kind and I'm sure this is as much a shock to her as us."

"I can wait a while if you need company." John said.

"No. I think I'll go home and freshen up. They'll have to reschedule because this is highly irregular. Fred has a lot of explaining to do."

On cue, a police car pulled in through the gates.

"I am so sorry Daphne's ceremony was messed with. And thank you."

With that, Ilona sprinted down the hill toward the car park. John headed back to Daphne.

WHERE IS EDWINA?

"Porter and Browne are here." Zeke announced.

Daphne's head shot up. As common as her real maiden name was, it still always made her look. Gave her heart a little lift in case this time... She pushed down the hope. The trouble with pushing away hope was that one day, it might not reappear. But when one discovered their birth certificate had the wrong information on it, and eventually found out what their real surname would have been under different circumstances, well it changed a person.

Two police officers cut through the cemetery, a thirty-something woman, and a fifty-something man. As they neared, Fred rebuttoned his shirt and fixed his tie. His forehead was beaded with perspiration, which Daphne put down to standing in the direct sun for too long. The afternoon was warm enough for a bit of sweat.

Thanks to the efforts of Fred's staff, most mourners had left or were leaving. The ambulance was gone and Daphne's thoughts went out to the woman inside it. One minute Petra West was chatty and enjoying rhubarb jam and then she was so ill that an ex-doctor recommended a priest.

The revelations from Tracy and Amanda were both odd and concerning. Daphne filed their comments away.

Just in case.

"I'm here, doll. Are you doing alright?" John reached for Daphne's hand.

"Yes, but I don't know what I should be doing." Daphne tugged at his hand. "Let's find some shade."

An expansive flowering tree provided instant relief. And more privacy.

"I spoke to Ilona." John said. "Drink some water, Daph. You look so hot."

Although she knew what he meant, a bubble of mischief —fuelled by a roller coaster of emotions—rose and she couldn't help herself.

"You'd better believe it, young man."

With a wide grin, John put his arms around her and planted a kiss on her lips.

"Ouch! Scorching!"

They both smiled. Forty plus years of marriage created a comfortable and safe place to co-exist, and Daphne loved John as much—if not more—than the day she'd married him not long out of high school.

The moment passed and Daphne sipped on her water, eyes on the events unfolding around the fallen casket. The police officers squatted to take a look as Fred had, while he stood by, running his finger under his collar.

"Do you think Fred had anything to do with the—er—mix up?" John asked.

"I'd like to say no. But he has some serious questions to answer about this, being the funeral home director. And he is so nervous."

"Losing a client would be nerve-wracking, I imagine."

"How could it happen though? And why. Actually," Daphne glanced at the discussion underway between Fred

The Shadow of Daph

and an officer, "the why is what interests me. Unless it was a complete error and the wrong casket was collected, then a person, or persons, did this deliberately."

It was a dreadful thought. Best not to dwell on it.

"You said you spoke to Ilona? She was upset with Fred."

"A few tears but she seemed better after we spoke. Not as distraught." John said.

Tracy and Zeke stood a little away from the casket and were deep in conversation, with Zeke's eyes darting back to the casket as he spoke. Fred's other staff were nowhere around.

From the other side of the grave, Sonia stared at the casket, or the people around it. It was too far for Daphne to be certain. The laughter was gone. There were no tears. In fact, nothing but a vacant stare. Edwina was still her mother and instead of the funeral being almost over, she had this new shock to deal with.

Fred nodded in Daphne's direction and the older police officer headed their way. The younger one took photos of the casket.

As he neared, the officer removed his cap and stepped into the shade with a smile.

"Bit warm out there today." He held a hand out to Daphne. "Adam Browne. Leading Senior Constable but Adam works."

"Nice to meet you, although the circumstance could be better." Daphne shook his hand. "This is John, my husband."

As the men shook hands, Daphne took a closer look at the officer. He had a pleasant face with a ready smile and warm brown eyes. He was completely bald and wore glasses.

"Not what you expected when you agreed to officiate?" he grinned and took out a notepad. "I've no wish to keep you standing around so just wanted to ask a couple of questions, if you don't mind."

"Not at all. I have some myself."

The corners of John's mouth flicked up. Daphne ignored him. He knew her too well and no doubt had already figured out she wasn't about to leave the poor mourners without some form of closure. As long as Edwina could be found, of course.

"Would you run through the events of today? Anything you observed, particularly concerning the casket or the hearse. Or the funeral home. Fred mentioned you were there twice today." Adam said.

"Yes. I met with Fred, Sonia Drinkwater, and Tracy Chappell, to go over the ceremony and discuss the final wishes of the deceased. We spent about an hour in a room in the funeral home. When I was leaving, I met Ilona briefly. But none of the staff at that point."

"Aside from the gravity of the situation, did anything strike you as unusual, or of concern?"

Daphne considered her role as a celebrant to be similar to any professional caregiver. Doctors, counsellors, lawyers, clergy. In some circumstances in a life, a person might say or do something they wanted kept private. Times when emotions ran high. It was a mental balancing act to know when to share what she'd seen and heard. Apart from her chat with Ilona, there'd been others present. Others who would be questioned as well. Nothing to keep a secret.

"Sonia was very upset. Angry. Mostly at her mother which is quite normal under the circumstances."

Adam nodded. "Normal for Sonia. She isn't afraid to speak her mind."

At least her behaviour was unremarkable. No need to get into her comments about being pleased Edwina was dead.

"In that case, then nothing felt out of place. When I returned this afternoon, on Fred's request, I met a number of other people. Apparently, the pallbearers were having a little meet up first."

"Who was present?" Adam wrote in his notepad.

"Fred. Tracy. Desmond Rogers. Zeke. Sorry I don't know his surname. Poor Petra West. And Amanda Sinclair."

Did I just recall all those names? Go me!

Adam glanced up. "Amanda was there?"

"She arrived last."

"But she wasn't a pallbearer." He made a note. "Any observations about that part of the day?"

Let me think.

Petra getting stuck into the food early. Tracy not wanting Amanda to have a glass of champagne. The tray dropping after a minor accident. Cross words spoken. Zeke cutting himself.

But is any of it relevant?

"I got the impression Amanda wasn't welcome there by some people. But I'm a stranger to town and funerals are times of great stress for those involved."

"You are a discreet person, Mrs Jones." Adam said.

"Please call me Daphne. I just had a thought about Petra. She told me—at the funeral home—that I should try the rhubarb and apricot jam on a scone and that she just had. I do hope that isn't why she fell ill. Food poisoning. Or something worse."

"Something worse? Such as?" Adam put away his notepad to give Daphne his full attention.

Back in Little Bridges, after the events at the wedding she'd officiated, Daphne had tried to tell her suspicions to the police officer who'd been first on the scene. It had been less than successful, leaving Daphne feeling she was not being taken seriously, or worse—that her observations were of no value. This was different, because the body in question was deceased before Daphne and John arrived in town. But what if this otherwise pleasant officer also considered she should mind her own business?

Her throat tightened up.

As if he could read her mind, John gently took her water bottle from her hand and undid the lid before giving it back with a soft, "Have a drink."

Grateful for the minute to think and her husband's sensitive response, Daphne sipped.

"It might be a while before we get an update on Petra West, so I'll ask Fred to put aside the—rhubarb jam?" Adam asked.

"Rhubarb and apricot jam." Daphne corrected "I'm sure I'm only speculating but what if something's wrong with it."

"Not much for rhubarb but I imagine other people are." Adam said. "Best to be safe."

His quiet agreement boosted her spirits a little.

"What will happen now, Adam? Who is looking for the deceased?" Daphne asked. "Is there anything we can do to help?"

Adam's phone rang. "Might be able to tell you in a min. Be right back." He wandered off, answering as he walked.

Fred, Zeke, and another of Fred's employees worked in unison to roll the casket onto its base. The other police officer was speaking with Sonia who had her back turned to the scene. There was nobody else around.

"Daphne, John. Thanks for waiting." Adam slid his phone into a pocket as he rejoined them. "That was the funeral home. I've asked them to locate and quarantine the jam in question. There's been a search of the premises and unfortunately, no sign of the deceased. There are no unaccounted for caskets and no other clients." He ran a hand through his non-existent hair. "I'm heading over there now and Fred can come with me. Bodies don't just disappear."

John spoke. "Are we good to go back to our caravan?"

"Yes. I'll grab your contact details in case I need to follow up with any other questions but for now, please try to enjoy our little town. The agricultural show begins this afternoon which is always fun."

After swapping cards, Adam returned to the grave. He spoke to Fred, whose shoulders visibly dropped. The other police officer was finished with Sonia, who'd moved into some shade and sat on the grass. Her eyes had rarely left the casket anytime Daphne looked her way.

"Should I go and see if she needs to talk, John?"

"What if we go home. Give you a chance to freshen up and take a breather. A cup of tea."

Tea did sound nice. Being somewhere away from the shock of the last hour sounded even nicer. This funeral wasn't over. They'd find Edwina. And reschedule. And as long as it didn't interfere with the wedding she was heading to, she'd be ready to help Edwina go to her final resting place.

As long as they can find her.

SIDE TRIP

"Tea is ready." John called as he carried the pot to the table in Bluebell. Two cups and saucers were already in place as well as some lemon tarts he'd found in the fridge. Daphne had barely eaten today and with all the upset at the funeral, a little treat wouldn't go astray.

"Lemon tarts! Good idea." Daphne slid behind the table. She'd changed into what she often called her 'cosy' clothes—three quarter length loose pants and a pretty blouse. She looked much more comfortable like this than her suit on a hot day, as smart and professional as it was.

John joined her at the table and poured the tea. "What an afternoon!"

"Indeed. And I have a feeling this will keep us here longer than expected, so apologies in advance."

"There is nothing to apologise for, Daph. What are the odds of something like this happening?"

"About the same as the events in Little Bridges. We went there for the sole purpose of me officiating a wedding and ended up staying far longer thanks to the treacherous behaviour of people who had murder on their minds."

Daphne picked up one of the tarts. "You should see all the food laid out at the funeral home for the wake. No tarts though."

"When you were talking to Leading Senior Constable Browne, I got the feeling you were being careful what you said about the pre-funeral meeting." John poured some tea. "I imagine in a small town where everybody knows everyone, there are old rivalries as well as friendships, and losing a valued member of the community might bring out some ill feelings. And I didn't mean to make that pun."

Daphne nodded. "Well, somebody *did* lose Edwina, quite literally."

For a few minutes they sipped their tea and each enjoyed a lemon tart. Cars filled with families periodically drove past Bluebell along the dirt track. Perhaps to visit the show which was beginning today.

"That hit the spot." Daphne said. "What you said earlier is true. As much as I want to help, I'm rather worried about saying too much. It isn't as though there's been a murder or anything, just a missing body. And an ill woman, of course. But apart from wondering if poor Petra was affected by something in the jam, I really don't know if anything else that happened has anything to do with Edwina's disappearance."

"I'm sure you would say if you had suspicions."

"I would. It was just a bit odd when Amanda Sinclair arrived." Daphne's brow furrowed. "She seemed hesitant about coming into the room but muttered something in response to Tracy's toast. And it wasn't very complimentary to Edwina. Tracy was quite scathing to Amanda when the champagne glasses ended up on the floor."

John opened his mouth to ask what happened just as her phone beeped. He closed it again as she read the message.

"It's from Fred. Says police have a lead on Edwina and can

we stay for a possible rescheduling of the funeral for tomorrow, pending the outcome."

"That's positive. Say yes, of course. We were going to be here tonight so if this is resolved then you'll still get to fulfil your appointment." he reached over the table and took one of Daphne's hands. "I know how important it is to you. Finishing your job."

"I hate to think of someone not being properly laid to rest, not to mention what her friends and family are going through with all of this."

And because you are driven to make those around you happy.

"Another cup of tea? Then, how about a visit to this show in Shady Bend?"

When they'd returned to Bluebell earlier, Daphne had glanced at their bed with a small sigh. She was tired. They'd only been travelling for a few weeks and she wasn't quite accustomed to the nomadic life they followed. Although there was much to enjoy about visiting a new place once or twice a week, there were moments she longed for more stability again. A bit less unpredictability.

Be adventurous, Daph!

She managed to sweet-talk herself into a better frame of mind and now, as John found a parking spot among rows of cars in a paddock, she found herself looking forward to the rest of the day. The agricultural show was held on a large sports ground surrounded by bushland. According to the sign as they'd driven in, the show had only opened an hour ago and would end at midnight on Saturday. The air was filled with music and laughter, along with some excited squeals from people on carnival rides, as she and John headed to the main entrance.

"Quite a few people already here." John had changed into shorts and a shirt and wore the floppy white hat he favoured wearing when fishing. "Can't remember the last time we went to a show."

We haven't. Not together anyway.

"I think you took a couple of our foster family over to the one in Green Bay." She said. Her heart was beating a bit too fast and she slid her arm through John's. "What shall we do first?"

"What if we see what's on in the main arena and then plan it all out? Looks like its straight ahead." John paid for their tickets and accepted a small booklet which he slipped into his top pocket.

Arm in arm, they followed the road past old buildings on one side and the entry to the carnival on the other. Country agricultural shows in Australia were an old tradition from the times of farmers and growers competing for more than pride of what they produced, but to find new markets and showcase their animals and goods to buyers. Over time, entertainment in the form of travelling side shows—carnivals—became a common addition which was anticipated by young and old alike in towns often too small to offer much entertainment.

"I do love seeing the horses." Daphne said as the main ground opened up ahead. On perfectly manicured grass, which wouldn't stay that way for long, three rings were marked with temporary roping. In one, judging was underway of a breed of cattle. Led by white coated handlers, the group of red cattle stood calmly as a trio of judges made notes. Another ring was empty, but the third was set up for show jumping and riders without their mounts, walked the course.

They stopped in the shade of a grandstand and John took out the booklet.

"Let's see what's what." He opened it up to a map and then squinted around the ground. "All the buildings around the perimeter are in use. There's a cat show, oh, but that doesn't begin until tomorrow. Livestock apart, there are woodchopping competitions a bit further along from here. They run pretty much every day with the grand final on Saturday. There's an art show."

"Like the sound of that."

"Agree. There's the craft pavilion which has items for sale. And the food hall. Local produce. Baking competitions. Preserves and the like."

What had Tracy said earlier today? Preliminary judging started today.

"I think we should check it all out, love. Not like we have to be anywhere."

They doubled back for a few metres then turned left onto a wide and busy hard dirt path. Families, couples, and groups of teens bustled along in both directions, occasionally stepping aside to allow a horse and rider cross, or make way for an official vehicle to slowly nose through.

The sting was leaving the air as the sun dropped behind the tall trees, making the late afternoon air pleasant. Behind them the music and screams were less intrusive as they put the grandstand between themselves and the carnival. Daphne rotated her shoulders. The carnival wasn't going to hurt her and this was a good opportunity to send whatever old memories had emerged right back where they belonged. Hidden.

"Art show first?"

"Perfect."

After stepping through the open double doors of a stone building, Daphne and John stopped for a moment for their eyes to adjust to the darker interior. There was a hush in here reminiscent of a library. Of the few people wandering, most wore official's vests. The room was split into art in its different mediums, and a section at the far end which immediately took John's attention. Photography.

"Hope you don't mind if we wander down there first?" John was already on his way.

"I'll catch up."

John's interest in photography was a growing passion as he recorded their journey in images. More and more he was experimenting with different techniques using apps on his phone. It all was above her understanding, not because she wasn't smart enough to follow what he did, but because it wasn't fascinating to her as it was to him.

Much as she tried to show her interest, he would enjoy the exhibition more on his own.

She gazed around. Along one side were large easels holding canvases with oil paintings. A table was filled with smaller easels and lots of watercolours. And another table displayed miniatures at one end and an eclectic mix of entries at the other.

The oil paintings ranged from quite stunning to less than ordinary, but Daphne believed art was in the eye of the beholder. It was just that some didn't appeal to her. Perhaps she'd been spoilt over the years, for Rivers End—their home for many years—had two talented artists, Martin Blake and his grandfather, Thomas. Martin specialised in abstracts but was just as capable of producing wonderful portraits. Thomas was known for his emotion-charged seascapes. Haunting work which was sought after even decades after he'd completed it.

Almost at the end of the row was a painting of a woman. It wasn't particularly well executed—in Daphne's opinion—but it was interesting. The woman was staring in a mirror. She was older. Perhaps in her sixties, hair piled on top of her head in a neat bun and her eyes serious. Even angry. Her reflection though smiled back at her, the eyes alive with love and happiness. Quite the contrast.

"As conflicted as the woman herself."

Daphne hadn't noticed anyone close by and turned to the man standing to her right. Desmond, leaning on a cane.

"Hello. How is your ankle?"

He grimaced. "Hurts. But just a bad twist thanks to Miss West."

Rather than point out that Petra was hardly in a condition to have deliberately harmed him when she collapsed, Daphne gestured to the painting.

"Someone you know?"

Desmond snorted. "Yes. My painting, not that it matters or will win anything. Should have entered it into the Archibald instead."

Australia's premier art award might be a bit out of the league of this piece, but there was clearly more to this than Desmond's throwaway comment. Something about the woman was familiar. The expression reminded her of someone she'd met. Someone much younger.

"There's a lot of love in this painting, Mr Rogers. And if you painted it, then you certainly portray some intense feelings for the subject."

Eyes back on Desmond, Daphne sensed a tension in the man. His mouth was in a straight line, lips hard together. And a muscle in his cheek twitched. As though he was considering her assessment, he stared at the painting.

"You are seeing something that isn't there, Mrs Jones. My neighbour she was, but I had no love for the woman."

"This is Edwina?"

He nodded. "This is Edwina."

ART, OR ARTFUL?

Edwina Drinkwater—or at least, her likeness according to Desmond—was an older version of Sonia, once Daphne took another look with the new information. The same eyes, at least the angry ones.

"Have you been her neighbour for long?" she asked.

"Too long. Decades."

"I am curious." Daphne turned her back on the painting to address Desmond. "I'm being personal, but why paint her if you didn't get on with her?"

Desmond shrugged. "She was two faced and it appealed to the artist in me to capture it in paint. Edwina hated it. Told me I shouldn't have taken her image without permission and she'd sue me if I showed another soul." He suddenly flashed a row of ragged teeth in a rather fearsome smile. "Thought she'd blow a fuse when I said I was entering in this and every art show I could get to."

"What about Sonia? Does she agree with her mother?"

"She doesn't agree with anyone. But I think she quite likes this painting." Desmond took his phone from a pocket. "Another message. Group chat never ends."

Daphne looked at the painting again as he tapped on his phone. There was a detail she'd not noticed before. The background was faded out a bit but looked like shelves and a counter. A shop? And perhaps those were jars on the shelves. In the reflection was a narrow bottle like one for sauce but it wasn't replicated where it should have been.

"Whoever thought they knew where she'd gone to was wrong." Desmond announced.

"Where Edwina is?"

"Stupid idea to go off looking in the bush. Who'd drag a body out of a casket and leave it lying around under a tree?"

"Is that what they thought?"

"Police got an idea this was some kind of prank. Youngsters having a bit of fun but why would they even bother. Not easy to pick up an embalmed body let alone carry it any distance." He shuddered. "Edwina was probably rejected by the afterlife, rose from the dead, and is on her way home."

Before this conversation became any more macabre, Daphne excused herself and went to find John. As she wound her way past the tables, a familiar sensation raised the hairs on her arms, and she glanced back. Desmond leaned on his cane with both hands, his eyes following her.

Browsing the collection of photographs made John happy. He was surprised by the depth of quality in the entries and returned twice to an image of an old cottage. The house was unloved, in need of paint and repair. But the gardens were spectacular and immaculate. Not a weed in sight and manicured lawns with a sweeping path between long beds filled with flowers and trees. He was taken by a long garden bed of roses alternating red, pink, and yellow varieties. Very striking with the riot of colour against the drab exterior of the house creating an interesting contrast. Something loved. Something neglected.

Judging was complete for the photographs and this one had placed but not won its section. He compared it to the winning entry, a nice enough image of a tree but without the attention to detail of the other one.

I still have much to learn.

Daphne was on her way to meet him but she glanced over her shoulder and he couldn't help but look in the same direction. The older man from the funeral, the one who'd hurt his ankle, stared at Daphne.

His stomach tightened. Something about the man's intensity bothered John. Daphne always knew when someone was watching her and she'd obviously glanced back thanks to her intuition. Something was off about this whole day, between odd behaviour from mourners through to the dropped casket and missing body.

"John? You look worried."

"That man. Did you speak to him?" he asked.

"Desmond. Yes, he was one of the pallbearers and hurt his ankle when the casket fell. And yes, he was watching me walk over here." Daphne took his arm. "Have you seen enough of the photographs?"

"Feeling a bit hungry, actually. Shall we find some food?" John was happy to leave this building and they found a food truck outside and got on the end of the line.

"He painted Edwina." Daphne said.

"Sorry?"

"Oh. Back there I was talking with Desmond. I'd been looking at a painting of a woman and he told me he did it. And that he was no fan of hers but they'd been neighbours for decades."

Maybe he stole her body to get back at her for something.

"So, he didn't like her but did a painting of her." He pushed his unkind thoughts away.

"Said it showed how conflicted a person she was. She was looking in a mirror and the real Edwina was stern and angry but the reflection was happy. But you know what I think?"

They moved forward as people were served and left the line.

"I got the impression that whoever painted it had a strong emotional attachment to the subject, but when I said that Desmond scoffed at the idea. I think he once loved her. Perhaps still does."

They ordered hotdogs and chips and returned to the main field to eat. The show jumping was underway and the grandstand was almost full of spectators but they squeezed into a row near the front. One by one, horses and their riders navigated the arena in a timed competition that left people gasping and clapping. The food wasn't as good as the entertainment and Daphne only finished half of her hotdog.

"Bit on the cold side." She dabbed her lips with a napkin.

"Sorry. We'll make up for it with a nice restaurant meal in the next couple of days."

"I'm not complaining." Daphne took his hand as they headed away from the grandstand. "Besides, we might find some goodies in the produce pavilion."

Evening was closing in and enormous overhead lights powered up with a series of crackles. Further past the art show they located another building, this one up a long ramp and with lots of glass windows. At the entrance, a table was set up with free goodie bags and a smiling woman handed one to each of them.

"Well, this is nice." Daphne said. "Which way should we go?"

"Daphne! Over here."

A female voiced boomed from the far wall.

The Shadow of Daph 49

"Tracy." Daphne didn't sound very enthusiastic but now the woman was bustling towards them it was too late to pretend they hadn't seen her.

Talking to Desmond was one thing, but Tracy was a different matter.

Be nice. Ignore her sharp tongue. Move on quickly.

She was enjoying her visit to the show with John and hadn't considered the woman might be here.

Tracy wore a mid-length brown skirt, long boots, and cream blouse and over that, had a vest with 'Official Judge' on a rosette pinned on the front. She carried a clipboard and was heavily made up. Even at the funeral she'd been less dressed up.

"Daphne, Daphne. I hope you've got some news for me."

"News?"

"Well yes. I'd imagine Fred would let you know first when the rescheduled funeral will be." She frowned. "Guess it means Edwina is still missing in action. Whoops. I mean, inaction. Better not let anyone else hear me joking about it."

That was a joke?

"I saw Desmond a short while ago and he had news that there was no progress from the police. Something about a group chat?" Daphne said.

"Never understood why someone his age is messing around on social media. I can only imagine what Fred did with her but he'd better find her fast. All of this right in the middle of the biggest event of the year is terribly inconvenient." Tracy grumbled.

Daphne was lost for words. A woman had died and then been removed from her casket by persons unknown. It might have inconvenienced Tracy but it had done a bit more to poor Edwina.

"Anyway, we must do our best to go on. Come and see what I've been doing."

Without waiting for a reply, Tracy strode to a series of long tables. They were set up with multiple levels and on each were individual displays of bottled goods. All had their lids off and a sample of the wares was on a small side plate. Each was numbered and there were handwritten labels on all.

"This competition is always fiercely contested. Until now." Tracy waved an arm dramatically in the direction of the jars. "All of these are from within our own region and use fruit or vegetables from this area, so it is seasonal. There are jams, chutneys, even locally made mustards. And preserved lemons, baby cucumber, cherries…the list goes on. And my job is to select the top three."

"You said 'until now'? Is something different this show?"

Tracy rolled her eyes. "Well, obviously. No entries from Edwina so the competition is fairer. At least as far as the sauces go. And the grand prize."

John wandered along the table, inspecting the display.

"Sauces?" Daphne had no idea what the woman was talking about.

"You must have heard about her secret recipe?"

"Only something Ilona mentioned. But no, I have no idea about a secret recipe."

Tracy laughed. "Edwina would be turning in her grave. Whoops. Too soon? Anyway, she imagined her sauce was world famous and kept the recipe hidden so it wouldn't be stolen. But it doesn't matter, because the absence of her sauce means other people have a go at winning, even if they don't deserve it."

"I see numbers, so each entry is anonymous?" Daphne

asked. There was some delicious looking apricot jam which made her mouth water. As long as it didn't include rhubarb.

"Of course. We couldn't have competitors claiming I was prejudiced in my decisions. Mind you," she leaned closer to Daphne to a conspiratorial whisper. "I've judged so many of these competitions that I could probably guess who made what. Good thing I'm not open to bribery."

Good thing nobody overheard you.

"I'm sure everyone would consider you a fair judge. If you've been doing this for so long, they must value your expert opinion." Daphne said, her eyes drifting back to the apricot jam.

Tracy nodded. "Yes. Yes, I'm well respected. At least by most people. Edwina never liked my decisions but she wasn't nearly as good in the kitchen as she believed." She looked over Daphne's shoulder. "Speaking of people whose creations aren't as good as they think…hello there, Sonia. Have to say I'm surprised to see you here."

For the first time, she agreed with Tracy. Sonia was last seen sitting alone under a tree. What a traumatic day she'd had and from Daphne's observation, there was little in the way of comfort offered to her from the other mourners. Not even from Fred, who'd earlier revealed an almost fatherly side when he'd counselled her to calm down. He'd been caught up with his own troubles, of course, but still, was there nobody at the funeral who cared enough to check the daughter of the deceased was coping?

"Haven't you finished judging yet? Or whatever you call judging. People want to know who won."

Sonia was dressed in the same clothes as the funeral—black knee length dress, black tights, and black ankle boots. Her skin was tinged pink, no doubt from sitting in the sun for so long. She didn't bother to look at Daphne or Tracy but gazed up and down the table.

Tracy huffed, clutched the clipboard against her chest, and stalked to the opposite side of the table where she glared at Sonia.

Daphne's heart thumped.

I'd like to tell you both to be nice. It's a difficult time.

Her phone rang and she couldn't grab it out of her handbag fast enough. She stepped away to answer.

"Mrs Jones, this is Leading Senior Constable Browne. Adam."

"Oh yes. How are you? I mean, is there any news?"

"I'm fine thanks. And the answer is yes. And no."

"I see. Well, not really."

John joined her and she mouthed 'Adam' to him.

"We did have a lead earlier which hasn't panned out. It probably was a long shot but we'd had a tip off and it was worth following up." Adam said.

"Do you mean the one about local youngsters playing a rather bizarre prank?"

He chuckled. "Small towns. Can't keep a secret. Although the whereabouts of Edwina Drinkwater is one secret I wish would make it to the Shady Bend grapevine. The main reason for the call is to see if you mind answering a few more questions. In the morning will do, assuming you and your husband aren't planning on leaving before then?"

"The morning is fine. Shall we come to the police station?" Daphne asked.

"If you can. I'll send you a text message with the address. Any time between nine and eleven is great, but if I end up having to attend anything I'll let you know."

They chatted for a minute then Daphne disconnected the call.

"Adam wants to ask a few questions in the morning. I imagine he's trying to fill in the gaps."

"So, no success finding the…er, missing person?"

"Not yet. Do you think we can slip away?"

"Let's try." John took her arm and they zigzagged between displays and people through the pavilion.

Once they were a safe distance away from where they'd been, she risked a look back. Tracy and Sonia were talking. Their body language was no longer angry, in fact, if Daphne hadn't seen so much animosity between the women today, she'd have thought them to be friends. Close friends. Sonia even smiled as she spoke with animation and Tracy patted her arm.

Adam wasn't wrong about small town secrets. From the odd behaviour of several residents today, Shady Bend had its fair share.

A FEAR FROM THE PAST

After another hour of sampling cheese, buying some local wine, and indulging childhood memories with popcorn, they were more than ready to head back to Bluebell.

With the coming of night, visitors spilled through the gates at a rapidly increasing rate until the pathways and road filled with excited faces and laughter. Teenagers grouped together and they might have been the loudest, but they also stepped aside to make room for prams and the occasional wheelchair. Daphne smiled at them. She'd loved being a foster mother to children but really enjoyed having teenagers in the house. There was something special about watching a child grow into young adulthood.

"And then they disappear." She said under her breath.

John turned his head to look at her, a question in his eyes. Hopefully, he hadn't heard. She didn't want to tell him where her thoughts drifted to some days. Her wishful thinking about reuniting with some of their foster children. One in particular.

He squeezed her hand. "We seem to be a long way from the gate. Want to cut through the carnival?"

"Oh. Um, sure." It wouldn't be so bad. There was an almost straight path from where they were now to the road they'd come in on. A Ferris wheel towered over the carnival where ride attendants shouted above music blaring from one ride after another. People lined up at food trucks and rides alike. Lights flashed in time with a procession of recorded silly voices at a shooting range.

"Here, I'll carry your bags." John took the handful of sample and show bags from Daphne and added them to his, then offered her his free hand. "Fancy going on the Ferris wheel?"

"My, oh my. No thank you. Just the idea of being all the way up there is enough to make me dizzy."

"Sorry." John guided them past a fire breather who'd gathered a small crowd around himself. "We've never been to a carnival or anything together and I don't really know why. I always went as a kid. My parents even took us kids to Melbourne Royal Show one year." He grinned. "Never forgot how big it was. Could fit ten of this size shows into it. Twenty. And the showbags were so expensive we were only allowed one each and boy, did we spend our time making those choices."

"Sounds fun."

This was taking a long time, walking through here. Her spare hand moved to her chest, pressing against it. And for some reason she was having trouble swallowing.

"Daph?"

People milled around. The music was loud. Perspiration dripped between her shoulder blades.

"Daphne. Doll, are you alright?"

Why did John sound worried? She smiled at him and nodded.

Get a grip, Daph.

From ahead, a different tune cut through the crowd

where painted horses bobbed up and down and around. The music must be the same for every carousel on the planet.

She stopped, her mouth open as she fought for air that just wouldn't reach her lungs.

"Okay. Something isn't right. Are you unwell?" John turned to face her, still holding one of her hands. "Or is it the side show?"

Daphne nodded.

A flicker of a smile crossed his lips. "With the absence of a definitive answer I'm assuming it is the side show."

She nodded again. Her words weren't coming out and if her heart didn't stop thudding so hard, she might fall in a heap right on this spot.

"We can turn back." John scanned the area around them. "Actually, I think we can get behind all of this. Looks as though the fence is just the other side of these tents and at least then we're away from the bulk of the noise. Give it a go?"

He didn't really give her much choice, just gripped her hand more firmly and set off between two food trucks. She held on for dear life. Because, if she lost him…

"Ah. Just as I thought. Step over the cables on the ground. I can see a path through."

True to his word, in a few minutes they were at the boundary fence. It was a relief to stop here, away from the chaos of the carnival. It was still noisy but in the darkness her heart slowed to normal and she swallowed.

John ran his hand over the mesh fence. "This is temporary fencing. Let's see if we can find a gap."

Daphne giggled.

"No giggling, young lady. We are escapees and must find a way out before we're caught." John's voice was stern, which only made Daphne laugh harder. He followed the fence in oversized steps, slightly hunched and darting his head from side to side. All they needed was some comedic spy music. "Aha! We don't even need those giant bolt cutters you keep in your handbag. Or explosives in your pocket. Just let me move this a bit…" he carefully lifted a panel. "And we can slip through before anyone sees."

It didn't take long to step through the space and then John replaced the panel. Without another word, he picked up the bags he'd dropped on the ground and then her hand. The night was lit by an almost full moon which was just as well with the lights of the show behind them. They were on the grassy field not far from the carpark and that is where they headed. Only when they were both in the car and John was pulling out of the carpark did Daphne let out a long sigh.

"I've got you." John reached over and patted her leg. "Never let anything bad happen."

Daphne opened her mouth to say he couldn't be with her every minute but clamped it shut again. Instead, she covered his hand with hers until he needed it for the steering wheel.

Being married to someone for decades teaches you about two important people. The person you married and yourself. John had no doubt Daphne was the reason he was the man he was proud to be. Her unwavering belief in him had seen him through plenty of tough times and gave him confidence to start their real estate business all those years ago. And he'd become the trusted agent people came back to time and again from watching how she encouraged clients to talk about what they needed, rather than wanted.

Today he'd discovered something new about Daphne. A fear she'd hidden their whole lives, if indeed she even knew it existed before tonight. So, he needed to listen when she was ready to tell him what she needed. And somehow not speculate in the meantime on the reason she'd turned white and looked ready to flee when they were at the carnival.

"I might check my website, love. See if there's anything pending for me." Daphne carried her laptop to the table. "Can't afford to miss a query."

"In that case, I might update our blog. And can I pour you a glass of red wine to finish the evening?" He was already taking wine glasses from the cupboard over the sink and fancied opening one of the bottles they'd picked up at the show.

"Yes please. Have you got some new photos for Bluebell's Blessings?"

Since beginning their travels, John had created a blog for their friends which was getting quite a following. He wrote about each town they visited, highlighting interesting details and adding any funny experiences as well as images he was happy with.

"I have. Was up before dawn this morning and got some interesting shots. I'll show you in a few minutes." He opened the wine and poured the deep red liquid into the glasses. "Anything on your website?"

"There's a query from a couple in Minyip. Why does that sound familiar? Anyway, they have their wedding set for one week before Christmas. What do you think about me accepting?"

John brought the glasses over and sat opposite. "No reason why not. We can leave early the next day and be back in Rivers End that night for our Christmas preparations. And Minyip is familiar because it's been a location for television and movies. In fact, it would be great to visit so can we make sure we're there a couple of days early to do some touristy things?"

Daphne's eyes lit up. "Of course! And now we'll have some time to rewatch some episodes of the Flying Doctors ahead of visiting because I'm sure now that was filmed there. What a treat."

They raised their glasses. "To Minyip!"

For a few minutes they worked on their respective laptops. Daphne was typing rapidly with a smile on her face and she finally had relaxed her shoulders. Talking to her clients always made her happy and he exhaled a breath of relief. She glanced up and tilted her head with an unspoken question.

In response, he lifted his glass. "Are you enjoying the wine?"

"It is yummy. I've told this lovely couple I'd be honoured to officiate their wedding and directed them to the next part of the process, so that's me done for the evening. What about you?"

"There's a comment here from the last blog entry which I thought you'd like to hear. It was the one about you helping solve the crimes in Little Bridges. Shall I read it?"

Daphne closed her laptop, picked up her wine glass, and nodded.

"How thrilling to hear the outcome of what must have been a scary time for the people involved. Be proud of yourself, Daphne, because you made a difference. But, please, dear friend, try to stay away from danger because you are so special to those who know you. All our love, Elizabeth and Angus."

There was a sad smile on Daphne's lips when he looked up again. "Oh, I'm sorry. I thought you'd like to know our friends are keeping an eye on us from afar."

Elizabeth White and Angus McGregor were close friends of theirs who ran Palmerston House, a beautiful old home-turned-bed and breakfast, in Rivers End.

"I'm not sad. At least, I don't want to. Sometimes I realise how far we are from home and I miss it. I miss them." She took a quick sip. "And I'm going to do what they say. Not get into any dangerous situations again."

Something told John she was talking about more than avoiding killers. Her eyes were on her glass, not him. There was a tremor in her tone that only he would ever pick up. What had spooked her at the show?

"I'm pleased to hear you say that. With all the events of today, I'm hoping things are quickly resolved and we can resume our journey to the next wedding."

"We are in complete agreement." She raised her glass. "To resolutions."

Long after John had fallen asleep, Daphne stared at the ceiling, her arms hugging her body and her thoughts racing. She'd wanted to talk to John about what happened at the show but had nothing to tell him. Some long-forgotten moment from her childhood had been unleashed by sights and sounds she'd hidden away and none of it made sense yet.

But I won't go back to the show. I just can't.

As for getting involved in the fallout from the funeral... no, she wasn't going to do anything except answer the questions the police wanted to ask and hope Edwina's funeral could go ahead very soon. She'd had quite enough of solving crimes and was going to put it all out of her head and get some sleep.

She turned onto her side and closed her eyes. Today had been far too long and too stressful.

You're safe now. John is here. And you can sleep.

She'd make pancakes for breakfast with some maple

syrup. She shuffled a bit to get more comfortable and let her mind reach out for slumber. All was quiet.

Tap.

Tap. Tap.

Her eyes opened a little. A tree branch touching the roof?

Knock, knock, knock.

That wasn't any branch. John stirred. Surely nobody was at Bluebell's door at this time of night?

"Daphne? Are you in there?"

Swinging her feet over the side of the bed, Daphne reached for her dressing gown and found slippers for her feet. The voice sounded familiar and before she could call or knock again and wake John, she wanted to see who was there.

She peered through the kitchen window. A shadowy figure was outside in a long, billowing dress. Daphne hurried to the door and swung it open.

"Ilona? Are you okay?"

Tears streamed down the other woman's face and her long hair was a tangled mess. Daphne climbed down and put her arms around her without even thinking. Poor Ilona. Had something else happened to make her awful day even worse?

"Daph?" John was at the door, rubbing his eyes. "What's going on."

"Ilona is here. Come inside, dear. We'll get you some water."

A couple of minutes later, Ilona was seated at the table with a box of tissues and glass of water, while John and Daph sat opposite. Ilona wiped her eyes with a handful of tissues and then drank the whole glass.

"I'm so…sorry to just turn up. I might be wrong, but I felt a real connection with you, Daphne. I feel we could be friends. And John, you were so kind earlier." She glanced from one to the other and then gulped. "I've had news. Terrible news."

Daphne and John exchanged a glance. Had Edwina been found and something dreadful happened to her remains?

"What is it, Ilona?" Daphne asked.

"It's Petra. She's dead."

A CHANGE OF HEART

Daphne gasped.

Ilona nodded, her eyes brimming with tears again.

"That *is* terrible news." John said. "Do you know…well, what caused it?"

"It had to be a reaction to the new medicine she's been on for her immune disease. There's no actual information yet. But I blame myself. I should have been there at the pre-funeral meeting. If only—"

"Now you listen to me, Ilona," Daphne patted Ilona's arm. "Unless you made Petra ill then you have nothing, not one little thing, to feel bad about."

"But there might be."

"Might be what, dear?" Daphne asked.

"Something to indicate foul play. Isn't that what you sleuths call it?" Ilona pulled a handful of tissues from the box and blew her nose.

John's eyes met hers. Sleuths? Seriously?

"Not sure we're following. Would you like more water?" John was on his feet and had picked up her glass before she answered.

"Oh, yes. I'm parched. Let me start at the beginning. Well, not that I know if it is the real beginning but as much as I know. Petra is more than she appears. She always has been and I've known her for a good ten years or more since I moved here from Little Bridges. Despite being so sweet and bubbly, there's another side to her and not everyone liked it." She accepted the refilled glass from John with the flicker of a smile.

"What kind of side?" Daphne asked as John sat again.

Ilona glanced around as if checking for eavesdroppers. "She liked to know what everyone was up to. A gossip. And lots of people like to talk about what's going on but she took it to a whole new level by keeping a list of what she called misdeeds. And if that wasn't stupid enough, she told people she was doing this!" She lifted her glass. "At first there were some arguments, particularly at the RCCC, but then most people just ignored her."

"Ilona, do you think Petra was blackmailing anyone with what you called misdeeds? Would someone have meant her harm over their secrets?" In Daphne's experience, people sometimes killed for much less. If Petra's death was suspicious, on the same day Edwina's body disappeared, then something was terribly wrong in this little town. And hadn't Fred mentioned something about a recent scandal?

Despite the hour and the long day she'd had, a small rush of energy perked Daphne up. This might well be a mystery worth exploring.

"Well, if they did, then it will be someone among us. One of those she kept tabs on. Or at least, that's my take on it. Edie always said Petra West was trouble, but that was mainly because she once owed Edie quite a bit of money. For that matter, she was always borrowing ten dollars here or twenty dollars there and somehow all of us indulged her even though she rarely paid us back."

A potential blackmailer who also owed money all over town. Petra West—according to Ilona—was a different person from the one Daphne met. But some people were very good at hiding their true selves.

John, with his cautious nature, wasn't as impressed. "Probably best to wait for the official results before anyone speculates."

He was right. Which sparked a question.

"I know this is a sad subject for you, dear, but with Edwina, Fred mentioned she passed away from natural causes. Would you mind sharing what happened to her?"

After taking another handful of tissues, Ilona nodded. "Nothing so dramatic as with Petra. She was gardening. At home. Apart from her shop, her garden was the big love of her life and she would spend hours out there, even until it was almost dark sometimes. Anyway, Fred went to visit the other night and couldn't raise her at the house. Sonia wasn't home either and for some reason he walked around the garden." A tear dribbled down her cheek. "There she was. Peacefully sitting on the ground against a stone wall. Gardening gloves still on. And deceased. She'd been diagnosed with a serious heart complaint a few months ago which she didn't broadcast and the doctor said it was a heart attack. Never even got to say goodbye."

Silence fell. Ilona dried the tears and stared at the table. Daphne wasn't sure what to say. The other woman's grief was contagious and Daphne's heart hurt for her. How awful for Fred to find Edwina and not even be able to render assistance.

"I really should go and let you both go back to bed. I'm sorry I disturbed you but I just needed..." Ilona stood with a sad sigh. "Although I like living in this area, there's nobody else I could talk to. Not now Edie's gone."

"Are you okay to get home?" John opened the door.

"Thank you, yes. I only live a short walk away and the fresh air will do me good." Ilona stepped onto the ground.

Daphne followed. "We can walk with you."

"Please, no. Besides, you are both in night wear and I don't want to inconvenience you more than I have."

"Then please take care. But can I just ask…was it normal for Fred to visit Edwina at night?" Daphne asked. "They were friends?"

"Friends? Not really. They used to be married."

Married. Which must be why Sonia listened to Fred at the funeral home.

"Sonia is his daughter?" Daphne asked.

"Maybe." Ilona walked away. "Nobody knows for certain. Good night."

Daphne wasn't certain if she'd slept or simply drifted in her thoughts during the hours until dawn. What she did know was there was a mystery tugging at her and depending on the outcome of her visit to the police station, she might have to delve into it.

She got up when John woke and they had a quick coffee together before he wandered off with his phone to take some photos. It was a pity they weren't near a waterway as he loved to fish and it helped him relax.

While John was out, Daphne opened a new notebook she'd recently bought. Her other one was almost filled with a mixture of the notes she always made before a ceremony, and quite a lot of pages dedicated to the events in Little Bridges. It was time to start fresh.

First though, she whipped up pancake batter and put it aside while she sliced a punnet of strawberries. The maple syrup bottle was almost empty so at the last minute she'd toss the berries in some butter and sugar and drizzle what was left over the top. And more coffee. Everything was ready to begin cooking so she took a few minutes to make some notes.

She titled the first page 'Edwina'. Some instinct told her the deceased woman was central to the subsequent disappearance of her body and the passing of Petra. But it was a long stretch of the bow to connect how.

"Start with why, Daph."

Why would someone remove an embalmed body from its casket before burial? She chewed on the end of the pen until she noticed what she was doing and wrote instead.

A prank
To hide something
To cause distress/payback?
For evil purposes

Daphne wasn't about to consider what those evil purposes might be.

"I'm back." John swung the door open and climbed up. "I smell strawberries."

"You do. I've made a pancake batter."

"Perfect." He dropped a kiss on her hair. "I see you are making a list. Keep going and I'll freshen up and cook while you write."

"I don't expect you to cook!"

He didn't answer until he returned a few minutes later. "I enjoy flipping pancakes. And you can talk to me about your thoughts while I do."

How did I find such a good man?

John heated the crepe pan and tossed some butter in. "Quite a shock about Petra. What do you think?"

"I have the strongest feeling her death is connected to Edwina's disappearance. And I was trying to work out why her body went missing." Daphne read out what she'd written. "Anything I've missed?"

"Ilona said Petra collected information about people. Bad information. What if Petra, or even a third party using Petra's notes, forced someone to do it?"

Daphne wrote down 'blackmail'. "Still doesn't give us an idea of who it might be."

"Not yet." He poured batter and gave her a quick smile. "If there is a crime behind any of this, I imagine you will put some ideas together. What about the other people you've met? How do you view them?"

Good question. "Bit early to rate them as suspects because we don't even know if—or what—crimes have been committed. But I have formed some opinions."

John didn't say a word and Daphne had to smile to herself. He knew her so well.

"I think a few locals have something to hide. Fred. Sonia. Amanda. Tracy. And Desmond. Mostly him so far because he is hiding whatever compelled him to paint Edwina against her wishes. On the other hand, Ilona means well but her grief is clouding her judgement, I feel. She's seeing things that might not be there."

"Quite a few people with something to hide. Should I do something with the strawberries?"

Daphne slid out from behind the table. "Those pancakes look fantastic. Just toss the strawberries in some more butter and a spoon of sugar. I'll get our plates."

When they sat down to eat, their plates were pretty as pictures.

"Thank you, John. I love having breakfast with you in Bluebell."

"Me too. Have to admit I'm enjoying our nomadic life even if it does seem to lead us to some strange events. Events which I thought you said you weren't getting involved in."

True. But Ilona's revelations intrigued her. She picked up her fork. "I'm not."

"So, what about your notes?"

"Them? One never knows when the written word will come in handy. But mark my words, we'll be out of this town before you know it and then those notes will be relegated to a page called 'never happened'."

QUESTION TIME

The police station in Shady Bend was an old stone cottage converted into one large room with two desks. There were a couple of closed doors which might have been a kitchen and bathroom or even an interrogation room, but none had signs. Between the front door and the main room, a wall had been removed and a counter added, along with a locked access door.

At least, it had a lock but when Daphne and John arrived, the door was propped open with an old boot.

"Come in." Adam was finishing a phone call at a desk and gestured to two chairs on the opposite side. "Right. That's very helpful. Yep. Ring me once you know." He hung up and smiled. "Thanks for coming in. That was regarding Petra West and I'm afraid the news isn't good."

"She passed away."

Adam leaned back in his seat. His brows raised.

"We had a visit last night from Ilona with the sad news." Daphne said.

"Ilona told you. Interesting. Did she happen to mention where she got her information?"

John shook his head. "She was pretty upset and didn't mention it. Do you have the cause of death? I mean, only if you are allowed to say."

"No. Yeah. Toxicology isn't back. Thinking it's some kind of reaction or overdose, whether intentional or not and perhaps a prescribed drug. Which is one of the reasons I appreciate you being here early. With this development, I've got some questions about Petra as well as Edwina."

"Most happy to help." Daphne said. "Can I ask a question?"

Adam straightened, pulling his chair closer to the desk. "Go ahead."

"What do you think happened to Edwina?"

He grimaced. "Wish I knew. We have tracker dogs on their way and will do a proper sweep of the bushland around the funeral home. At least it might give us an idea if she was carried on foot for any distance or put into a car."

"Any theories?" Daphne pressed.

"That is two questions. But no, I'm not at the theory phase. Still at the 'what the heck happened' with a dash of 'what possessed someone to do this?' phase." He grinned and put his fingers on the keyboard. "My turn. I've been busy asking a lot of questions, but they've been of people who live in the town and knew Edwina. Most were close to her one way or another and either in a state of shock or hiding something. Too early to tell. So, your take on the day might insert some much-needed clarity."

"Where would you like me to start?" she asked.

"Can you go back over what you've already told me from when you arrived at the funeral home? From the first meeting."

"I had a mid-morning appointment with Fred, Sonia, and Tracy. The purpose was to go over the ceremony I'd drafted based on information sent through by Fred in a message.

Due to the short notice, I had prepared a fairly generic document so was looking forward to having some input from Sonia because of her relationship to the deceased. We were in the funeral home in the reception room. There was some discussion about people who wished to speak at the funeral —Tracy, Desmond, and Ilona. And the last wishes of the deceased." Daphne said.

"Which were?" Adam asked.

"Gifts to the mourners who attended the wake. I believe they were from her shop. A table was prepared filled with bottled goods, small pieces of artwork, framed tapestry and the like."

"Ah. I saw the table at the funeral home." Adam stopped typing to look at Daphne. "Did you see Edwina? Was it an open casket?"

Daphne shook her head. She'd have not wanted to view her if it had been open. "My understanding is there was no viewing."

Was she even in there?

"Adam, Ilona mentioned last night that Edwina was found in her garden. Nothing suspicious as she'd had heart problems for some time. Was there any kind of police involvement?" Daphne asked.

He reached for a file and flicked through. "Fred found her, realised she was deceased, and called her doctor. After examining Edwina, the doctor signed a Cause of Death certificate, which was straightforward and indicated natural causes. No need for us or even an ambulance. And Fred, being our only local funeral director, took care of everything else. Sonia would have been informed and approved Fred being responsible for her mother. Or there may have been a pre-existing arrangement."

The phone on the desk rang. "Sorry. Be right back." Adam answered as he walked to the back of the room.

John touched Daphne's shoulder. "What are you thinking? I can see your brain ticking over."

"Just gathering data."

"As long as you don't find yourself knee-deep in someone else's problems."

She knew what he meant. The last time she'd got involved in helping solve a murder she'd ended up putting herself at risk. Not that the events in Shady Bend were linked to any murder.

Unless Petra's death was intentional by someone else's hand.

Daphne forced her face into what she hoped was a reassuring expression. "Don't own any long boots so best to stay out of knee-deep situations. Do you think there's something familiar about Adam? He reminds me of someone."

"Funny you mention that. I got a sense I'd met him from the beginning. Must have one of those faces."

Adam returned and dropped into his seat with a sigh. "Sorry about that. Trying to get a bit more help up here but we're such a small town we rely on the bigger stations in surrounding towns for numbers and there's a blitz on the highway underway. Might be able to pull a couple of officers off it to assist but in the meantime, it is me and Constable Porter until the dogs and handlers arrive."

"Can we help?" John asked. "Never mind taking a walk in the bushland."

Daphne hid a smile. So much for staying out of things.

"Very kind of you to offer, John. We've already had a civilian sweep of the area but will keep you in mind if we need extra legs and eyes. When do you both intend to leave town?"

After exchanging a glance with John, Daphne spoke. "It depends on when I can perform the ceremony. I would like to speak to Fred about the possibility of holding it regardless of Edwina's whereabouts but I'm not certain on the protocol and have no wish to offend."

With a short laugh, Adam returned to the keyboard. "Guarantee you will offend someone in Shady Bend regardless of your intentions. I've worked in quite a few places in my time and this one takes the cake for being contrary. Nice people but they work against each other a lot of the time."

Daphne filed that away as Adam continued.

"But you have another appointment coming up?"

"I do." Daphne chuckled. "At least, *they* will say 'I do'. I just tell them when to say it. And yes, in four days I have the great honour of marrying a lovely couple in Benalla. We have to leave by Friday morning in order for me to meet with them on Friday afternoon."

Hands off the keyboard, Adam tilted his head as he looked at Daphne. "You have a pretty special job. I know a few celebrants and usually they stay close to home. As Ilona does. Makes sense really as there is always something happening to keep her and those like her busy. But you get to travel as well. And bring—I imagine—your own special brand of love to those who need it."

Oh my.

"She certainly does, Adam. I've known Daphne since high school and there is no other person I know who seems to understand what a person is going through and finds exactly the right way to comfort or support them. And while I would rather she only does happy ceremonies, the care she gives to those grieving is something to behold."

Although the wonderful words warmed her heart, they also made it hard to speak.

With a quick smile, Adam returned to the keyboard. "Back to my questions. You finished at the funeral home. What was next?"

She licked her lips. "Ilona was waiting for me outside the funeral home to have a quick chat about her speaking at the funeral. Then no sooner had we got to Bluebell than I got a call from Fred. He asked if I would go to the pre-funeral get together to meet the pall bearers. So, after a quick lunch and change of clothes, I arrived to find the room transformed for the wake."

"With the table?"

"Yes. All the gifts on a central level and lots of food around the sides."

Adam stopped typing to flick through his notepad.

"You mentioned who else was there. Fred. Zeke. Petra. Tracy. Desmond. Amanda." Adam read his notes from their chat at the cemetery. "Amanda wasn't a pallbearer. Earlier, you suggested a feeling she wasn't welcome. Why is that?"

"She stood outside the door at first, then came in."

Amanda had said something odd when she'd thought nobody was close by. Something in response to Tracy's toast. The words evaded Daphne but they'd been uncomplimentary. With nothing concrete, there was little point mentioning it.

"And there was a small incident between Tracy and Amanda, more of an accident." Daphne said.

"Go on."

"Tracy was carrying a tray with glasses of champagne. I declined to have any, I mean, with such an important ceremony ahead it wasn't appropriate. But Amanda said she'd like one and when Tracy walked away without giving her any, there was a mishap and the tray was dropped."

"Mishap?" Adam stared at her.

"Amanda tried to help herself and the tray overbalanced. Petra cleaned it up. Tracy said something about trying to avoid a disaster and Amanda always finding a way. Oh, and Zeke tried to help but cut himself and Petra sent him off to clean it up. It was an accident but I got the impression Tracy was annoyed Amanda was there."

Yet again, the phone rang. After this call, Adam grabbed his keys from the desk. "Apologies. Dog squad is at the funeral home so can we continue this later?"

A few more minutes and Adam drove off after locking the station. Daphne and John stood on the footpath. Across the road was a café and without so much as a glance at each other they crossed over. If there was one thing they both needed it was a coffee and a chat.

TRUTH IN TALK

"This was a brilliant idea, love." Daphne stirred her coffee and smiled across the table. "Needed to have something to pep me up a bit after the interrupted sleep last night."

The café was almost deserted with only one other customer at a table and one person serving. Looking through the window, John saw the odd car drove by but the street wasn't as busy as he had seen previously.

"I wonder where everyone is."

John grinned. "I was thinking the same thing. Seems a bit on the quiet side. Are you sure you wouldn't like one of these pastries?"

She shook her head. "You go ahead. I'm fine."

"What if we find somewhere nice for dinner tonight? Can't see us leaving today so we might as well enjoy the local fare." John suggested.

"I would love that. Although Shady Bend isn't on the map for its culinary delights, I have a feeling it is under promoted. After what we saw at the show, I'm excited about trying some of the locally made products."

There was movement across the road near the police

station as a car pulled up and immediately, a couple climbed out. Both were in jeans, T-shirt, and peaked caps which were pulled down over their eyes and they were too far for John to know if he'd come across them. And it wouldn't matter, except for the way they huddled together part way along the path to the station, looking past each other and back to the road. Not looking. Checking.

"Are you wondering what they're up to?" Daphne asked.

She was also watching the couple, her long fingernails tapping the handle of her coffee cup. Something about the events in this town warned of coming trouble. Not for them, but among the residents. So many at odds with each other and such tension now that one of their own had disappeared and another had died. Daphne wouldn't be able to let go.

"I am. Do you recognise them?" He asked.

"I think the man is Zeke. He works for Fred. The height and build is right but I can't see his face or hair. But the woman is Tracy. I'm certain."

After another check around them, the man scurried to the station, his head down. The woman returned to the footpath and gazed one way, then the other. At the station door, the man rattled the handle then disappeared around a corner.

Daphne had her phone out and was taking photos of them. The peculiar actions of the couple might be innocent, but John had the strongest feeling they were up to no good, and in a minute, he'd need to decide whether to call Adam.

A couple walking a dog headed towards Tracy and she pulled out her phone and spoke on it. She climbed back in the car and once the couple had gone past, the man raced to join her, sliding into the passenger seat.

"Not sure what we just saw. Looking for Adam?" John said. "Why are you screwing up your face like that?"

"That is definitely Zeke and Tracy. They were deep in discussion at the funeral after the casket fell and Petra collapsed. After the police arrived. He was edgy, kept looking at the casket. Yet Tracy was abrupt in how she spoke to Zeke at the pre-funeral meet. Bossy. Bordering on rude. And then there's the apparent dislike between Tracy and Sonia yet we both saw them laughing last night like best friends. Makes one wonder about what Tracy is up to."

It did.

Tracy got out of the driver's side and headed their way. Daphne was suddenly busy stirring her coffee again. If she wanted to avoid being noticed, it didn't work because Tracy saw them both through the window.

She pushed the door open with a bright, "Well, hello you two. Enjoying our little town?"

"Tracy! How nice to see you, dear." Daphne sounded welcoming and John had to admire her ability to make other people feel comfortable.

"Those coffees smell good. Back in a minute."

The minute Tracy stepped to the counter, Daphne leaned towards John and whispered. "Let's find out what she knows."

"Daph."

"It can't hurt."

There was little point objecting. Daphne had a look in her eyes. A glint of curiosity which he knew accompanied her love of puzzles.

"Right. I've ordered mine so might as well catch up while I wait." Tracy dragged a chair from another table and sat at theirs. "Nobody has found Edwina yet and Petra died. Did you know?"

John nodded, a little shocked by her indifferent tone. "We spoke to Leading Senior Constable Browne this morning."

"You did? Do you know where he is? Even better, where Porter is because I have information for her and the station is shut." She gestured across the road. "Don't want to sit around waiting."

Daphne's lips were pressed together and she gave John the faintest shake of her head. It wasn't their place to say. Not that it was likely to be a secret, but even so.

"No idea? I'll ask someone who does." Tracy tapped at her phone. "Did you have fun at the show? As a judge I'm disappointed so far. The quality of the preserves was particularly ordinary this year which isn't surprising."

"Why is that?" Daphne asked.

"Obviously because Edwina hadn't entered anything. Or she did, but it wasn't displayed posthumously. She generally won most categories and that irked the others." She laughed shortly. "The funny thing though is there has been a rumour lately that she didn't actually make any of them."

John feigned surprise. "Is it just a rumour?"

Tracy raised both eyebrows. "There's *always* truth in talk."

Daph's favourite saying.

"If that is the case, who did make them?" Daphne hadn't blinked an eyelid. In fact, she didn't take her eyes off Tracy. "And what did she usually enter?"

"Second question first. Preserved fruit, from her garden. Jams. With fruit from her garden. Oh, and she and Desmond swapped fruits as he has a decent orchard. Chutney. Her secret sauce. And oil paintings."

"Well, that's a bit different." John said.

"Never saw her paint anything and I always suspected poor Desmond did them for her and then the paintings he signed as his were inevitably beaten for best oil. Perhaps that is why he did that preposterous painting of her this time."

"Anyone else involved, or just Desmond?" Daphne asked.

A puzzled expression crossed Tracy's face. "It is a mystery. Not Desmond when it comes to bottling, but someone close to her. I'd say Sonia if it wasn't so funny. Petra was one of her fiercest competitors. And Ilona is useless. Maybe she got someone in another region to make them and passed them off as her own." She shrugged. Her phone beeped and she checked it. "Adam is at the funeral home with the canine team. Group chat has its upside. But he's not going to find her."

Daphne straightened. "I beg your pardon?"

"If our law-abiding, never-put-a-foot-wrong Adam wanted to find her, he would have already." Tracy pushed her chair back and stood. "I'll find Porter. At least she takes me seriously." She started to leave then turned back. "Oh, I was being sarcastic about Adam. He's crooked and I expect he had something to do with Edwina's disappearance."

With that bombshell dropped, she collected her coffees from the counter and left with a 'Cheerio' as she exited.

As much as Daphne had hoped to avoid Tracy, there was plenty to interest her from their conversation. It irked her that the woman believed Adam was crooked and she'd have liked to ask why.

John paid for their coffees and they set off for a walk around town, arm in arm.

The morning was getting a bit busier with a few more cars passing and it occurred to Daphne that it was still early. Not even ten o'clock. No wonder the place wasn't bustling. If it ever did.

"Shall we see what shops are here?" John asked.

"It won't take long, as the population is only about four hundred. I looked it up."

Beside her, John smiled and she squeezed his arm. "Thanks for your help with Tracy."

"Didn't do much."

"Sure you did, love. Asking her if it was just a rumour about Edwina not making her own goods. Have you considered acting? The surprise on your face was a sight to behold."

His smile turned into a lopsided grin. "You were pretty good yourself."

"Thanks. But she's right. There is always truth in talk. I've always said it. If you cast your mind back to when Christie first walked into our agency, I told her then there was speculation about her great aunt that deserved closer inspection."

"And I suggested it was old gossip to stay away from."

"And *I* was right." She smiled to herself. "Look at all the love and happiness which resulted from following the speculation."

John chuckled. "I give up."

"Besides, the world isn't filled with straight forward answers. The truth about a situation is often clouded by the passage of time or misunderstandings." Daphne stopped smiling. "Even by lies and deception. If everyone was truthful, we wouldn't need to rely on gossip or speculation." Her stomach tensed as sadness crept into her heart. "Why can't people be honest?"

John stopped them both beneath a tree and rested his hands on her shoulders. "This isn't about Shady Bend, or even Rivers End, is it, doll?"

She shook her head. If she answered, she might blurt out the words she'd kept buried for so long. It wasn't John's fault but if she brought up the past—that particular part of the past, he'd blame himself for not trying harder to help her find the truth about her family.

"Daphne Agnes Jones, my sweetheart. I'd give anything to help you find the truth. And I know we lost momentum thanks to building the business up. But the few occasions I've suggested we hire a private detective or the like, you've said no."

This was true. The shock of discovering the man on her birth certificate wasn't her father still resonated after all these years yet she'd come to terms with never finding her real dad. Too many roadblocks had stopped her original search. And the other loss, the foster child she yearned to see again, was another dead end. Privacy laws had to be respected.

"There isn't any point." Daphne whispered. "Sometimes it just hits me again but then I remember I have everything I need." She wrapped her arms around his waist and leaned against him. "I have so much to be thankful for. Our friends. Enough money to live a good life. Bluebell. And you."

John's arms held her tight against his chest and his heart pounded loudly.

"I'm really okay, John. I promise."

If only there was a way.

"And I think we should go and see if Edwina's shop is open." She gently extricated herself from the hug. "Instead of getting all silly, I'd like to gather some more information. Just in case."

There was doubt in John's eyes. She'd worried him.

"I mean it. I'm okay and we're okay. And I would love to track down some of the delicious looking apricot jam from the show last night." She said.

He took her hand. "We'll find that jam. And see what secrets are lurking within this shop of Edwina's."

LITTLE SHOP OF SECRETS

Without a doubt, *Edwina's Secret Sauces & Special Supplies* was one of the quaintest shops Daphne had ever seen. Built from bluestone, it had an iron roof painted dark red to match the timber window frames and door. Two windows were on each side of the door with inviting displays of products.

The door was open and aromas of dried herbs and lavender mingled with spices. It was enough to encourage anyone inside and Daphne and John didn't hesitate.

The interior was every bit as charming as the outside, with wine barrels set up as display tables and a counter made from recycled timber. The floorboards creaked with every step and in the background, a sound system played a track with tranquil raindrops then changed to waves on a beach.

"Oh, this is a darling little shop." Daphne said. "We might be here longer than planned."

"I think we might."

"Are those preserved lemons?" Daphne asked.

"They certainly are! And the best in the country if you ask me."

Daphne and John turned to see who spoke. A young

woman, mid-twenties at the most, slipped an old-fashioned shopkeeper's apron over her head and smiled as she tied the strings around her waist. Even her eyes sparkled as she crossed the short distance from a back room to where they stood.

"Welcome to the shop. I'm Constance."

"Nice to meet you, Constance." John said. "This is my wife, Daphne, and I'm John."

"Visiting Shady Bend for the first time?" she asked.

"Do we look like tourists?" Daphne smiled.

"Oh, I grew up here and have worked in the shop for years plus I have a great memory for faces. Don't remember seeing you before, although," she gazed at Daphne. "There's something familiar about you."

And you.

Constance had the warmest brown eyes in a pretty face shaped like a heart. There was a streak of red in her shoulder length dark hair. A bit like Daphne's. Which is probably why she seemed familiar.

"Is there anything in particular you'd like to see, or would you prefer to browse in peace?" Constance asked. "I can discreetly stand behind the counter ready to pounce at your command."

Much to her dismay, Daphne couldn't find any words. Her throat constricted and she nodded. What on earth was going on?

John jumped in. "Daph saw some apricot jam at the show last night. It looked delicious, so do you have any here?"

Constance grinned. "We sure do. In fact, we have over fifty flavours of locally made jam. Almost as many preserves, and yes, those are preserved lemons but they also have a special ingredient which is a touch of ginger. As for relishes and sauces…don't get me started." She hurried to a shelf and reached for a jar. "Apricot jam. One jar? Ten?"

Daphne laughed aloud and her mood shifted. "One will do, thank you. And one of the preserved lemons. What else do you recommend?"

"I recommend experiencing our tasting plate. What if I set one up for you both while you have a look around? Anything either of you are allergic to, or dislike?" With a jar in each hand, Constance headed to the counter.

"No allergies we're aware of, but I'm not keen on rhubarb."

"I'll be honest. Nor am I. Leave it to me and I'll find some goodies." Constance disappeared into a back room.

"You okay, Daph?"

"I am. Had a little moment when I felt a bit emotional but then I realised why. Constance reminds me of Belinda. Same delightful way of speaking."

Belinda was the daughter of one of Daphne's close friends in Rivers End, a bright and bubbly young woman who used to help her mother in the local bakery and now worked for Christie in her beauty salon.

John nodded. "I know what you mean. Both of them have such a friendly approach and don't mind being a little cheeky. Perfect for a shop like this. But I do have a question. Something occurred to me when Constance mentioned she didn't remember seeing us."

"Why wasn't she at the funeral?" Daphne asked. "If she's worked here for a long time for Edwina, surely she'd attend the funeral?"

"You'd think so."

Daphne and John enjoyed a few minutes browsing laden shelves, selecting a jar of plump cherries and a bottle of locally made olive oil.

"Right-e-o," Constance announced. "These are some of my favourites and are very popular." She placed a wooden board onto the counter. "There are three sweet offerings and three savoury. And a delicious little pickle that goes very well with the cheese I've added."

It was a good thing Daphne hadn't taken up John's earlier offer of a pastry. What a treat this was with tiny dishes with miniature spoons, a few slices of a hard cheese, and some small pieces of crusty white bread.

"Locally made bread. In fact, everything here is made within a thirty-minute drive of Shady Bend, so try a bit of everything." She collected some napkins. "I suggest a piece of cheese on the bread topped with the pickle. And then the same but with the other options. The sweet ones are lovely popped straight into the mouth. Oh, wait a min, I forgot something."

Constance vanished into the back room and in a moment emerged carrying an unlabelled sauce bottle. She poured a small splash of creamy, bright yellow sauce onto the plate and the aroma drifting up was something Daphne had never experienced. Sweet and savoury all at once.

"Dip a piece of bread in the sauce and tell me it isn't the best thing you've ever tasted."

Daphne did. The instant the sauce touched her tongue, layers of flavour played with her tastebuds. She closed her eyes to enjoy it.

"Told you. There's something special about this one. What do you taste?" Constance asked.

Eyes open and mouth sadly empty, Daphne considered the question. "Lemon but not too tangy. Honey but not too sweet. Something earthy. Reminds me of thyme. What is it?"

With a big smile, Constance nodded. "Correct on all three counts. But there are four other ingredients and depending on what the sauce accompanies, you'll enjoy other aspects of it. It goes beautifully with most vegetables but is also special over homemade ice cream."

John dipped a second morsel of bread into the sauce.

"Why haven't we seen this on supermarket shelves?"

"Oh. It's a private recipe." Constance said. "Not for mass production. I can sell you one bottle but we have to limit it as there are only a few bottles left."

"Yes, please. Does it have a name?" Daphne already had a sneaking suspicion. There'd been mention of a secret sauce and surely, this had to be the one. "And who is behind the recipe?"

Oddly, Constance blushed and turned her head away. "Um, I should get some water for you both." She collected two bottles of water from a fridge behind the counter. "The recipe belongs…belonged to the owner of this shop." She finally looked at Daphne. "The former owner. Edwina Drinkwater. She recently passed away so I'm not completely sure what will happen to the shop. Or the sauce."

"Dear, I need to come clean." Daphne said. "I was at the funeral. Edwina's. As the celebrant. So John and I visited here because other people said it was such a lovely shop and it is."

"Oh." Constance said. "You probably are wondering why I wasn't at the funeral. I had to be here. Nobody would tell me if I could go to it and Sonia said the shop needed to keep trading. So, I stayed here." There was a glisten in her eyes. "I'd have liked to be there. Edwina was good to me."

Daphne patted her arm. "As it is, you didn't miss the funeral. I expect things will resolve and I'll perform the ceremony and you'll have another chance to go to it."

Constance gazed at Daphne. "I have to do what is right for the shop, though."

"I'm sure if half the town is at the funeral, then you closing the shop for an hour won't be a big ask. Is Sonia taking over from her mother?"

"Probably not. Sonia doesn't like the shop very much but it does pay the bills. Most likely it will be sold. Tracy has always said she'd love to get her hands on it."

Another customer came in.

"Please excuse me, and enjoy the platter."

Daphne's phone beeped as her hand hovered over the plate and she reluctantly reached into her handbag instead of taking another bite. The morsels of flavour were enough to make a person want to stay here all day.

Not to be.

"John? Fred's asking if I can go to the funeral home to discuss Edwina."

He looked as reluctant to leave as Daphne felt. But he nodded. "Let's finish this though and buy what we want. Another few minutes won't hurt, surely?"

"You are a man after my own heart. No point leaving behind what Constance went to such trouble to prepare for us. What are you looking at?"

On the counter behind Daphne was a display of postcards. John's eyes kept going to one on the top row and Daphne turned to take a better look. It was an old house in a pretty garden.

"I saw this at the show. Much bigger of course, and I was struck by the contrast between house and garden."

"Oh, that's Edwina's place." Constance had finished with her customer. "Sonia takes nice photos and has the best ones made into postcards to sell. Edwina loved her garden a lot and when not here in the shop, was usually pruning, planting, or painting an oil of it." She took one and turned it over. "See, photo by Sonia Drinkwater. Here, have this one. There's a whole box out the back."

"That's very kind of you, but I will pay for it. Also, we have to meet someone so can we gather some goodies?" John asked, accepting the postcard with a smile. "Our visit has been wonderful."

"I'll find a nice big bag to put your many purchases in." Constance grinned. "What would you like?"

While John paid, Daphne took a quick look at a row of paintings near the door. On a higher shelf were oils on canvas without frames, each about the size of a paperback. The theme was flowers of many types from roses to sunflowers.

"Curious." She murmured.

"Ready, love?" John picked up a brightly patterned woven bag, laden with jars and bottles each wrapped in tissue paper.

"Constance, thank you for making our visit special." Overcome with a need to hug the young woman, Daphne managed to lift a hand to wave instead. "I hope we see you again soon, dear."

"Oh, me too! Please come back before you leave town." Constance picked up the board and sauce bottle. "You are most welcome any time."

Back on the street, John and Daphne retracted their steps to the car. The morning was warming up but not unpleasantly and the shops were busier. They made it back to the car before either spoke.

"You're very quiet, Daph. Feeling okay?" John put the bag into the boot.

"Me? Yes, yes fine. Deep in thought." She climbed into the passenger seat and waited until John started the motor. "Did you see the small oil paintings in the shop? A different flower in each one."

"Can't say I did. Why?" He indicated and pulled onto the road.

"Remember I mentioned the painting of Edwina that Desmond entered in the show?"

"The one where she's looking in a mirror and her reflection is different from her face."

"Yes. What struck me at the time was there was a lot of understanding, even love, in that painting but Desmond assured me he felt no such things for Edwina. I wish I'd taken a photo…there was a sauce bottle in it which was like the secret sauce bottle. And the style of the flowers—and I'm no expert—looked a lot like those in Desmond's."

"You think he also painted the ones in the shop? Didn't Tracy say as much earlier?"

"She did. But Constance mentioned painting as one of Edwina's great loves so what if, well, now I am being silly, but do you think Edwina might have painted the one at the art show?" Daphne doubted herself the minute she spoke. There was no reason for Desmond to claim it as his own. Was there?

By now they'd left the main street and were approaching the funeral home. Up ahead, a couple of police vans were parked along the road. Adam's patrol car was in the funeral home driveway. John found a spot under a tree.

"Quite a presence here. Would you like me to come with you?" he asked.

"If you don't mind. I'm not sure how long I'll be though."

"Doesn't matter. And to answer your question about that painting. If you think it is a self-portrait, would it explain why you felt there was some understanding and love woven into the paint? After all, nobody knows a person more than themselves, and Edwina might have had a strong sense of self. Just odd if somebody else put their name on it."

There were a lot of odd happenings in Shady Bend apart from a missing body and a sudden death. A secret sauce with no name and apparently nobody to make it anymore. A shop in limbo. Paintings done by one person, if she wasn't mistaken, but accredited to different artists.

"Better go and see what Fred is proposing." Daphne climbed out to a chorus of barking. "Let's hope that means the dog squad have found something."

INTO THIN AIR

The closer they got to the funeral home, the louder the barking. Partway down the driveway, one of the uniformed handlers had a magnificent German Shepherd on a tight hold as the dog strained to get closer to Fred, who was trying to talk over the noise to Adam.

John was a big fan of dogs and he'd thought a few times lately about suggesting to Daphne that they find a travelling companion. Loving them though didn't mean getting in their way when they were working, and the teeth on display from the angry dog reminded him this was a highly trained police officer. Not a civilian canine.

"Let's wait on the grass until we're called over." He and Daphne diverted off the path. "Fred seems to be the focus of our furry friend there."

"And doesn't Fred look upset about the attention!"

She was right. Fred glared at the dog and his hands were clenched. Fear possibly. And why was the dog upset? The handler leaned back on his heels, well in control of his dog and quite happy to let him bark. Something was going on which made no sense. Not yet.

Adam raised a hand to wave and Daphne responded with a big smile. She'd taken to the police officer almost on sight and John had seen how annoyed she'd been when Tracy made the comment about Adam being corrupt. It was a big statement and not a pleasant one. Daphne was an excellent judge of people and John trusted her gut feeling over anyone else's.

"Isn't he the most handsome creature?" Daphne nudged John.

What? Adam?

"Not sure if I feel the same, Daph."

"But look at his muscles."

Hadn't noticed.

"And the way he stands. As if he's ready to spring into action. One would never be afraid with him around."

John patted his stomach. He had to improve his fitness. Obviously.

"I know he's baring his teeth and looking all ferocious, but what a gorgeous doggie he is. Why don't we get another dog? Someone to travel with us?"

Oh. The dog.

With a chuckle at himself, John relaxed. "Happy to have a chat about it once we're back in Bluebell. And yes, he is a magnificent dog and a committed member of the police force."

The conversation between Adam and Fred ended. Adam joined the handler and the dog stopped barking, but watched every move Fred made as he headed up to John and Daphne. He glanced over his shoulder at the dog as he reached them.

"Thanks for coming on short notice. Sorry about that animal. No idea what got into it but it hasn't stopped trying to eat me since I walked outside."

"Have the police located Edwina?" Daphne asked. "There seem to be a few vehicles around."

"Not yet. The dogs can't pick up any scent, apparently. They've been through the funeral home and nothing took their fancy. Not even the food from yesterday which is untouched in the lounge."

Yet the dog was keen on Fred.

"Did they have something of Edwina's to use?"

"No idea, Daphne. All of us, the staff, stayed outside while the police went through with the dogs. Two of them are apparently searching down near the waterfall but Adam said they aren't picking anything up. As for that one." Fred motioned at the dog, who growled, "it must know I can't stand dogs."

John had nothing to say and from the way Daphne straightened her shoulders, neither did she. In his experience dogs were a good judge of character.

"Anyway, Adam says I can plan the wake. We can't do a funeral as such until this dreadful situation is resolved but at least we can fulfil Edwina's wishes and complete the wake. I'm going to speak to Sonia in a few minutes, but if she agrees, would you be willing to adapt your ceremony?"

"Yes, of course I can. I'll remove some of the parts more fitting with a funeral and emphasise the areas that remember Edwina. Is that what you have in mind?" Daphne asked.

He nodded. "Yes. And people can speak and get their gifts, eat, and toast Edwina. And then, even if the worst happens and her body isn't recovered, we'll have had a proper farewell and be able to move on."

Daphne pulled sunglasses from her bag and put them on. "Fred? Why wouldn't her body be found?"

"Just a bit strange that even the dogs aren't picking up a trace. But I'm sure it will be." He checked his watch. "If Sonia agrees and I can round everyone up, can we make a tentative arrangement for this afternoon? Let's say, four?"

"Fred, perhaps give Daph a ring once you confirm the

time." John asked. He had no intention of letting Fred expect Daphne to drop everything on short notice again like he had before the funeral. It wasn't fair for Daphne to have a guestimate rather than firm arrangements and a tentative time was just as likely to be moved at the last minute.

"Sure. Sure. I have to go and see Sonia now. Thank you."

Fred took a wide berth around the dog before going inside. Adam patted the handler on the shoulder and made his way to the grassed area. The handler and dog disappeared around the back of the building.

"Sorry about running off on you both earlier." Adam said. "So far we've got exactly nowhere with the dogs, other than the one you just saw taking exception to Fred." He didn't seem at all concerned about the mutual dislike.

"Is there any news at all? Was the funeral home broken into?" Daphne asked, removing the sunglasses she'd only just put on. "Do you think it might have been an inside job?"

Adam's lips flicked up for a second. "Inside job sounds very television cop show. But there was an unlocked exterior door. No idea how long it was unlocked and none of the staff can explain it and sadly, there is no video surveillance on the property. There's no evidence of anyone touching the casket apart from Fred, his staff, and the pallbearers but it had been polished the morning of the funeral so fingerprints might have been unwittingly removed. The dogs aren't interested. Almost as if she never even..." he pressed his lips against each other.

"Never even arrived here?" Daphne suggested. "Do you know for certain she did?"

"Zeke saw her. Paperwork checks out. And Fred is hardly about to pretend Edwina wasn't in the casket. There's no reason for it. No. I'm certain we'll find her in due course."

Daphne opened her mouth as though to say something but closed it and nodded. She glanced at John.

"We might get going, if you don't need us?" John said. "Daphne will be back here in a few hours so needs some time to prepare for the wake. Anyway, if there isn't anything else?"

"Not for now. I have to assist the search for a while, what if I touch base later so we can finish the interview?" Adam said. "Sorry to mess you both around."

He strode away in the direction the police dog and handler went a few minutes ago.

Daphne watched him leave. "Something isn't right, John. Call me suspicious, but I have a feeling there is a whole lot more to this than meets the eye. Too many secrets for such a small town. And so many questions. Shall we go back to Bluebell so I can write them down, love?"

"Now, first off, who else was involved in the funeral home's processes?"

"Processes? Is there time for a pot of tea?" John held the kettle aloft.

"Yes please! So, I'm not an expert and I really don't wish to sound clinical or be offensive, but what else can I say other than body? Deceased might work. Edwina sounds too personal." Daphne tapped the end of her pen against the fingers of her other hand. She had her notebook open at the table.

"Say whatever sounds right to you." John said.

"Okie dokie. I believe that a deceased person is collected by someone from the funeral home and in Edwina's case, probably from her home and by Fred with another staff member or even the doctor to help. The deceased undergoes the embalming procedure and is moved to the casket at the appropriate time. I'm not sure of the time frame for each of these but the funeral was supposed to be yesterday which was what...four days after she passed away. So not long."

"Not sure where this is going. Would you like a biscuit?"

"I think there are a few of my cookies left in the cupboard. Butterscotch if I remember correctly."

John glanced inside. "No. Must have finished them. There's a packet of those chocolate covered ones. What if we open them?" He grabbed the packet. "I know you think they're not healthy but it's only now and then."

"Once this wake is behind us, I'll do some baking. Much nicer to have my homemade cookies on hand. But store bought will be fine. I was sure there were some of mine in there."

John must have eaten them and forgotten to mention it. At least she knew how much he loved her baking and it was no trouble to whip up a batch.

Once John brought the teapot, cups, and a plate of biscuits over, Daphne added a quick note to the paper.

Who saw the deceased?

"I wonder if Adam has asked Fred who else was involved with the deceased?" Daphne helped herself to a biscuit. "That might narrow down the list of suspects and—"

"Whoa. Suspects? Daph, I'm sure the police have things well in hand."

"Going to disagree. Adam has *no* idea. An unlocked door but nobody knows anything about it. Police dogs who cannot pick up the scent of someone who was at the funeral home for several days. A funeral home director who stated he thinks Edwina won't be found. And then there's Tracy calling Adam corrupt. Questions over who is the real artist. And what happened to Petra West?" Daphne realised her voice was spiralling upwards and clamped her lips shut.

John leaned over and kissed her on the cheek. "I pity any

criminal who gets on the wrong side of Daphne Jones, celebrant sleuth."

Daphne giggled. She hadn't meant to get worked up but all it took was a couple of words from John and the frustration evaporated.

"Now, eat the biscuit while I pour the tea." John said. "I love how passionate you are about the truth. And I agree with everything you've said. Almost everything. But let the police do their job."

This wasn't anything new John was saying. Daphne had heard it more than once and in more than one situation. But while he was adamant about keeping her distance, more and more often he showed signs of being every bit as fascinated by small town secrets as she was. One of these days he'd have to admit he enjoyed putting puzzles together.

"I'll do my best, John."

His exaggerated sigh almost sent her into a fit of more giggles. She was little more than a kid in a grown woman's body sometimes. No point taking life too seriously. At least, not unless there's a murder involved.

SAYING GOODBYE

A few minutes before the wake began, Daphne put down her ceremony book to go in search of a glass of water. She'd been sitting in the reception room in a quiet corner to get things straight in her mind. Words were one thing, but making sure the emphasis was right was another. She'd spent much of the afternoon rewriting and finessing what she hoped was a memorable farewell for Edwina.

But not too memorable.

There was already plenty of negatives around the passing of Edwina Drinkwater, or at least, the aftermath and no doubt this would be spoken of for years to come.

The room was almost the same as when she'd been here yesterday. Goodness, it felt as though it was days ago, not just over a day. The perishable food for the wake was replaced with plates of fresh offerings but the raised middle remained filled-to-bursting with the now-familiar bottles and jars.

On one side of the room was a service door which she imagined—and hoped—led to the kitchen. It was where Petra had gone in and out of yesterday, and while Daphne had rehearsed, staff from the funeral home had been a steady procession from there to set up the table.

Daphne went through it into a long, poorly lit hallway with several closed doors on either side. At the very end was another door with a built-in window such as restaurants employ to ensure a safer way of entering and exiting their busy kitchens. Daphne peeked through the window in case someone was coming the other way.

"Oh my!"

There were only two people at the far end of the kitchen and they were in an embrace. Actually, more than an embrace. Full on smooching and hands in places, well, where they shouldn't be in public. Daphne was not a prude but a funeral home kitchen was no place for such antics.

One of them was Zeke and for an instant, Daphne assumed the other person to be Tracy. Despite the big age difference, they'd been seen together a few times and Tracy spoke to the young man with a familiarity a step beyond a working relationship. So, when the kissing stopped and the woman moved away from Zeke, Daphne had to slap a hand across her mouth not to gasp aloud.

Amanda?

Not your business, Daph.

She stepped back and turned away. Being seen watching them would cause embarrassment and might lead to questions about her own motives. No, best to return to the reception room and manage without water for now.

"Daphne?"

Dandelions and ducks! She'd taken too long to make a decision and been caught only a couple of feet from the door. Smile plastered on, she spun back.

"Hello, dear. I think I'm quite lost. Somebody said the kitchen was around here but I think all of these doors are locked." Not quite a lie. Or the truth. As if to prove her point, she turned the handle on the nearest door which wasn't locked and abruptly closed it. "Wrong room."

"Yes. That's where Fred keeps the embalming chemicals and protective gear. Not really a good place to be poking around."

Was that a touch of suspicion in Amanda's tone?

"The kitchen is behind me. Was there something in particular you wanted?"

"Glass of water. I normally keep a bottle close by but forgot to bring one."

With a sudden smile, Amanda stepped forward and linked her arm through Daphne's. "Why don't we go back to the wake and I'll get you a bottle of icy cold water? There's a stash of them in a fridge near the front desk and nobody will mind me getting one. After all, we can't say goodbye to Edwina without you."

Or without her body, really.

"Everyone is on edge." Amanda chirped away as if doing an update on the weather. "Fred is usually so calm but even he is snapping at people. Even at poor Zeke. I had to intervene."

Is that what they call making out these days?

Amanda continued. "But Fred calmed down when I said if we all stick together, we'll find Edwina. Even made the three of us a plate of scones to say sorry. And how much he appreciates our friendship and support under such awful circumstances."

Fred obviously didn't like upsetting people.

"May I ask you a question, Amanda?"

Amanda tensed, her arm tightening around Daphne's, but her voice remained cheery. "Ask away."

"When poor Petra collapsed, you said she'd need a priest…as if you knew she wouldn't survive. But what made you think that?"

They stopped close to the door back to the wake. Amanda stepped away, a hard expression entering her eyes. "You saw how she was. Short of having a stomach pump graveside, or an emergency response unit, Petra was a goner."

"Stomach pump?"

"Look. I shouldn't say this but the medical examiner will release the details at some point anyway. Petra had a condition and was trying a combination of new drugs. One of them had the side effect of—shall we say—lifting the spirits? My guess is being upset about Edwina, Petra took a couple more than she should to make herself feel better." Amanda said.

"I'm so sorry. You must have been a dear friend to know about her medication." Daphne fished.

Amanda screwed her face up. "Petra was a pest. Nice enough but she liked to be in everyone's business and wasn't above threatening to tell the community about what she'd dug up if you didn't loan her some cash or the like."

"Oh my! She sounds like a criminal. What if someone didn't like her making threats?"

"What. One of us killed her?" Amanda burst out laughing. "I can assure you we all pitied her. She was pathetic."

The door opened and Fred's head appeared. "There you are."

"Sorry, Fred. Just filling Daphne in on how Petra probably died." Amanda scooted past him. "I'll fetch you some water, Daphne."

Fred rolled his eyes. "Amanda has an over active imagination. Now, are you fine to start soon? People are arriving."

Daphne led the way. "Let's go and help everyone say goodbye to Edwina." There'd be time later to jot down these new revelations.

The ceremony went well. There were fewer mourners present than at the funeral, but they solemnly listened to Daphne, nodding in unison or breaking out in murmured agreement. People wore black with the same accent of colour requested for the funeral. Only Ilona looked different, with a shorter and fitted dress and braided flowers through her hair.

"The first person who wishes to speak is Tracy Chappell. Would you like to step up here, Tracy?"

Daphne moved to one side of the podium as Tracy worked her way through the mourners. She put a hand on either side of the podium and leaned forward. Was she about to unleash an impassioned sermon?

"Friends. And others. We are united by Edwina's passing. A few of us were close, dear friends of hers. Most though were only recipients of the wonderful wares from her shop, Edwina's Secret Sauces and Special Supplies. And speaking of her wares, I expect to confirm that I will soon be in possession of the recipe for her signature sauce and continue to make it in her tradition. Although a bit more commercially."

Constance was standing with Ilona and they exchanged a sudden glance. Tracy gazed in their direction and then focused on Desmond. More accurately, she smirked at him and his face reddened as he glowered back.

"But enough of me. Edwina put Shady Bend on the map for preserving. No town does it better and we prove it over and over by taking out so many awards around the state every year. If it can be preserved, bottled, sauced, jammed, or any number of other culinary techniques, then Edwina wanted it in her shop. We all knew Edwina as a tough businesswoman who stood up for what she believed. Even if it offended those around her."

"Tracy!" Fred whispered from the sidelines.

She rolled her eyes. "Righto. Time for me to let someone else speak. I'll miss the old girl. She might never have shared her secret sauce recipe with me until it was too late for her to see how successful it will be in supermarkets, but we had our good times. Hopefully, she'll stop hiding and hop back in her casket where she belongs."

A collective gasp rose from the mourners.

"Don't act all precious. Only saying what you lot would if you weren't so uptight. But while we're on the subject, if any of you have an inkling of what happened to her, tell Porter. And that's a wrap." Tracy stalked away from the podium to the back wall, leaning against it and taking her phone out.

Crossing her fingers that no other speaker would be so… blunt, Daphne nodded to Desmond.

He lumbered across the room, pushing his way through people who muttered and made space. At the podium he tugged on his tie to loosen it and wiped his forehead with a handkerchief. He sweated profusely. The room was uncomfortably warm with so many bodies in it and no air conditioning on but the staff didn't seem to notice.

For that matter, Fred had vanished. The door to the hallway clicked shut. Perhaps he'd had the same thought and gone to turn on the air con.

Desmond cleared his throat. "I am compelled to speak today. Should have been yesterday but some low-life took our Edwina from her rightful place. Here's a first. I agree with Tracy on this point. If you know anything at all, tell the police. Tell our Senior Leading Constable Brown. Or Constable Porter. But be honest." He dabbed his forehead again. "Edwina was my neighbour for decades and we might not always have seen eye to eye, but she was a good neighbour and raised a good kid." He scanned the room, finally resting his eyes on Sonia.

Daphne hadn't noticed her until now. Hair unbrushed,

her face was set and her eyes vacant with no repeat of the manic laughter from the previous day. Her clothes looked like she'd slept in them.

"Anyway, one reason I wanted to speak was to make something clear. Some of you believe I've tried to buy Edwina's property and that she refused, straining our relationship. I'm here to say our relationship, in the past year, was close and we made a certain arrangement after her heart condition was diagnosed."

All eyes were on Desmond. Even Sonia blinked and took a deep breath. Tracy lifted her chin.

"People believe Edwina never made a will. Always said she didn't believe in them. But she was clear on what she wanted to happen after her death and in respect to her house and land, it was that I am to have first option to buy it." Desmond nodded as if it was a done deal.

"That's a lie!" Ilona burst out. "Edie wanted Sonia to have a place to live for as long as she wishes."

Desmond shrugged. "Did I say Sonia would have to leave?"

People whispered to each other. Fred appeared through the main door, glancing around and then joining Tracy, who leaned close enough to say something. Probably catching him up on what he'd missed in a way only Tracy could.

This wasn't going to plan at all. Daphne approached Desmond and spoke for his ears only. "If you have any special words about Edwina, please feel free to say them. I'm certain there will be time later to sort out Edwina's wishes."

Daphne hated any kind of confrontation but wasn't going to allow the ceremony to veer any further off track. For a moment Desmond studied her face and Daphne's heart thudded uncomfortably, but then he nodded and addressed the room.

"I apologise if I've upset anyone. It is an emotional time

for us all. Just for the record, Sonia will always have security. And I will miss Edwina Drinkwater, even if she did believe she was a better gardener and artist than I."

He stomped away and people complained again as he pressed past.

"Our last speaker is Ilona."

Constance opened her mouth and Ilona touched her arm with a quick shake of her head. If Constance wanted to speak, then Daphne would make sure she had the chance, but it appeared as though Ilona didn't want her to. How strange. What was their relationship?

Ilona hurried to the podium and cast a sad glance at Daphne with a mouthed, *thank you*.

"Edie was my closest friend, but you all know that. For some of you, Edwina Drinkwater was simply the owner of a successful local business, a heavyweight in the culinary arts, and a respected, senior judge at many of this region's competitions. But to me, she was a warm and caring woman who put her heart into the community and would never turn a needy person away. And she did a lot to help the wildlife sanctuary. She leaves behind a beautiful daughter in Sonia, and darling, you made her so proud."

Sonia's eyes were on the floor.

"She also leaves behind the shop which has helped so many of us, either by being able to sell our products through it, or by enjoying its wares. Usually, a bit of both. I believe she had a different vision for her possessions than the ones mentioned earlier, but today is about celebrating Edie and I would like each of you to take a moment this afternoon to remember her in your own way." A tear ran down her face. "Goodbye Edie. I will never forget you."

As she made her way back to Constance, the mourners clapped and some touched tissues to their eyes. Sonia turned and left the room and a moment later, Tracy followed.

"Ah...um, would anyone else care to speak?" Daphne asked.

Ilona whispered something to Constance.

Nobody put their hand up or made moves to approach.

"On behalf of Sonia Drinkwater and the funeral home, thank you for attending today. Edwina requested all attendees have mementos to take home and I believe Fred is able to assist with this. Please spend some time here to celebrate Edwina's life and enjoy the delicious food and drink on the table." Daphne smiled and stepped away from the podium to a brief round of clapping.

She'd collect her bag and slip out and then, it was time to move on to a wedding. To a happier celebration.

PRESERVED

Back in the cemetery in Shady Bend, John stood at the spot where he'd been when he'd seen Ilona by the tree yesterday. Although he had a genuine interest in genealogy, there was more to his regular visits to cemeteries and graveyards than a hobby.

Daphne had another family somewhere. Her mother was no longer alive and her siblings lived on the other side of the country with sporadic communication, usually in the form of a Christmas card. It wasn't that they'd cut Daphne out of their lives, but the revelation that their father was not her father had raised many questions and the fallout of some of the answers changed everything.

Although Daphne rarely mentioned them, or the mystery of her birth certificate, it was a source of deeply kept sadness. Somewhere out there was her biological father, the one left off her birth certificate in favour of the man she'd grown up believing was her real dad.

John sighed. No point pondering the past. His goal was to find her father who somehow was invisible through the regular channels. No mention of him through the genealogy sites, nor even with Births, Deaths, and Marriages. He had some details thanks to Daphne's mother. A name. An occupation. And the frustrating knowledge the man had moved constantly around regional Victoria.

"Thank goodness for your new career, Daph."

While she performed amazing ceremonies, he researched and if she believed it was because he was interested in genealogy, then he let her. It wasn't a lie, but nor was it completely truthful. After all, if he couldn't find out anything to fill in the blanks in her life, then he'd never have got her hopes up.

This town was interesting. Tucked away off a main thoroughfare, it was an important part of a network of communities which shared resources. Apart from the produce, arts, and crafts, Shady Bend was known for its timber. Dense bushland surrounded the region but felling was part of a controversial history. These days, the unique flora and fauna was mostly protected, but fifty or sixty years ago, the timber trade had been considered respectable. And Daphne's father had worked in it, following the work from place to place.

John wandered from headstone to headstone. It was possible Alfred Browne was still alive so it was a sign of other relatives he sought. Alfred's parents or grandparents. So far, he'd found—and discarded—a dozen people called Browne since they'd begun travelling in Bluebell. Tomorrow they would leave Shady Bend and thanks to the bizarre events, he'd not been able to look for a local church where he often found old records.

"But there is Adam Browne."

All John needed was a couple of minutes alone with the police officer to ask a few questions. The man had mentioned he'd worked in other towns so might not even be a local but it was a chance worth taking.

His phone beeped as Daphne sent a message. He had an hour spare.

Going to the far side of the cemetery, John worked his way along rows, checking names on headstones. Many were related, as was so often the case with small towns where founding families expanded over generations.

He'd reached the final row before finding anything interesting. It was a small headstone and he had to bend down to read the engraving.

Moira Browne (nee Peters). Beloved mother of Constance and wife of Adam.

It was dated almost twenty years ago.

John straightened and wrote the information in his notebook. Constance had reminded him and Daphne of someone and now he knew, it was Adam. But Adam also seemed familiar and John couldn't work out why.

He glanced at his watch. Perhaps Adam would be at the police station and wouldn't mind a question or two.

"You're not leaving?" Ilona followed Daphne from the reception room. "I mean, why not stay for a bit?"

"I'd rather not intrude. The wake is for those who knew Edwina, dear."

"You must feel as though you do know her. Even just a little bit. Anyway, Constance has to leave and I'm feeling alone and it would be wonderful to have you around for a few minutes. If you could?" Ilona's eyes were intense. "And you are not intruding."

Daphne checked the time. John had made dinner arrangements in two hours but she wouldn't need long to change. "Let me just send a message to John and I'll be right in."

Ilona threw her arms around Daphne. "I'll make a little

plate of goodies for you." She was gone before Daphne could refuse.

"Not sure my jacket will stay done up if I indulge in those goodies." Daphne muttered as she sent a message to let John know she'd be a bit longer.

He replied straight away.

Am gainfully busy. Be there in one hour.

"Gainfully busy? What are you up to, love?"

About to follow Ilona, her attention moved to raised voices from another part of the funeral home. Women's voices in loud, angry whispers.

None of your business, Daph.

Nevertheless, her feet somehow carried her in the direction of the argument rather than back to the wake. A hallway led around a corner where a sign pointed to the restrooms. A bathroom stop was a good excuse if she needed one.

The entire building was made up of hallways, corners, and closed doors. Daphne peeked down a narrow passage where a single light bulb cast eerie shadows as it blinked on and off. An icy shiver ran up her spine and she gripped her briefcase close to her body before stepping into the middle of the hallway. Might as well be bold.

"You shouldn't have said anything. Not about the recipe!"

Sonia's voice stopped Daphne in her tracks.

"Oh for goodness sake." This was Tracy. "The sooner everyone gets used to the idea, the less risk there is."

"Risk? You've put my future at risk by blabbering about it. All I want is to live in my cottage and be left alone but now Desmond and Fred will be breathing down my neck trying to pry the recipe from my hands."

A long silence. Daphne made it almost to the corner.

"So, you do have it?" Tracy said. "All this time, you've led us to believe you don't know where it is—"

"What I know is nobody's business." Sonia's voice

faltered. "My mother kept her own secrets and now she's missing. Whoever took her has to be found, Tracy. It isn't right that she's not been buried."

Two sets of footsteps walked away. The women had gone.

"Unless she is."

Daphne spun around in shock. Amanda was behind her with a full-to-the-brim champagne glass in her hand and a peculiar expression on her face. Reminiscent of a child who has discovered where the lollies are hidden.

"Amanda. I didn't hear you."

"No. No, you were too busy eavesdropping." Amanda went past Daphne to look around the corner. "Not very nice of you. I'm beginning to think you were snooping around the kitchen before. Judging me for being involved with such a young man."

Best to ignore that.

"What did you mean? Unless she is?" Daphne asked.

Amanda drank half of the champagne in a couple of mouthfuls then flicked her eyebrows up and down. "Unless she is already buried. Somewhere else. Did anyone think of that?"

No. But now I am.

"Do you know something about it? Is this a rumour around town? In the group chat I keep hearing about?"

Amanda snorted. "Group chat. They kicked me out of it ages ago. Bunch of losers." The rest of the champagne went down her throat. "Do you know I was a respected member of a medical practice? Speaking of rumours, people like Tracy love to start them and keep them going. I've heard through the grapevine I lost my licence."

Daphne had heard it. "Not true?"

"Not true. I just choose not to practice anymore. Tracy loves dropping what she thinks is a bombshell but there is rarely any fact behind them." She touched her forehead with a frown. "Do you think it's hot in here?"

"Not here, but it was in the other room."

A couple of people from the wake went past chatting. Amanda leaned against the wall as if using it to prop her up and held one hand against her stomach.

How much champagne have you had?

"People didn't like Edwina. Only Ilona did, but she likes everyone. Tracy had an odd relationship with Edwina. Not friends but not enemies. Always trying to outdo each other with judging appointments and the like. As for Petra, she made a public accusation that Edwina was not making her own products. Jam in particular."

"What did Edwina say to that?"

"She threatened to sue. Got really nasty for a while with lots of sniping back and forth. Until Fred got in the middle of it."

"Fred? Because he was Edwina's ex?"

"I doubt that mattered. I think he was trying to win points in the hope of getting his hands on the secret recipe for her sauce. He came up with the idea of doing one of those blind tastings. Her jam against Petra's." Amanda rubbed at her stomach. "Scheduled as a fun event at the show, not that it matters now. Did you know Petra kept a little book filled with gossip?" Amanda raised the empty glass. Her hand was shaking. "Think I drank that a bit fast."

"Are you feeling alright, dear? Shall we go and sit somewhere?"

"Stomach hurts. Think I ate something a bit off. But I want to tell you about the book."

"What about it?" Daphne asked.

Amanda's face was turning bright red and sweat beaded on her forehead.

"She gave it to someone for safe keeping a couple of

weeks ago. One of the police. But it backfired and someone is using it for their own means."

"Wait, one of the police is using the information in Petra's book?"

"Who else would have poisoned Petra?"

Amanda slid down the wall. "This isn't from a dodgy sandwich."

Daphne dropped to her knees at Amanda's side. "Tell me what's wrong?"

"Me. I did something…wrong." Amanda's eyes fluttered shut and she toppled onto her side.

"Help! Someone, please help!" Daphne screamed.

It was like Petra all over again.

Flushed, clammy skin. Barely breathing. Unconscious.

Daphne draped her jacket over Amanda's torso. She hunted for her phone to call an ambulance as Fred ran around the corner.

"What the—" He skidded to a stop and grabbed his own phone. "Amanda! I'll ring the ambulance. Can you go and find Zeke? He has medical training."

"I should stay with—"

"No. No, I'll look after her." He reached a hand out to help Daphne up.

Her knees creaked as she stood and she grabbed her bag. "Where is Zeke?"

"Reception room. I think."

Daphne called John as she hurried.

"Ready early?" he answered.

"No. Yes. Its Amanda. She's collapsed. Same as Petra."

"Oh my goodness. Adam, we have to get to the funeral home." John said.

"Adam?"

"Sorry, Daph. I'm with him. Is an ambulance coming?"

"Fred said he'd call one but maybe call as well. In case he forgot." Or in case everyone in this town was out to get someone. "Please hurry."

She hung up as she entered the crowded room. People congregated around the long table and others sat on the stools in groups, some holding plates and others with champagne glasses.

"There you are!" Ilona appeared with two plates piled high with cheese, preserves, and scones. Daphne's stomach rumbled despite everything. "Would you like some champagne? There's plenty of bottles around."

Champagne.

Amanda had drunk a whole glass then collapsed.

Petra also had a glass yesterday and then collapsed an hour later.

"Everyone! Please, please give me your attention!" Daphne clapped her hands together and the conversations stopped as all eyes turned her way. "If you have champagne, I urge you not to drink it. Please put it down and wait until you are told it is safe to drink."

"Daphne? What on earth is going on?" Ilona asked. "I think you're scaring people."

She was. A number of people almost dropped their glasses in their rush to put them down. Others—including Desmond who took a long look at the bubbly liquid—held onto their glass.

"Does anyone know where Zeke is? We need some medical assistance."

"Zeke? Um, I think he's in the kitchen. But, Daphne, I don't under—"

Tracy appeared from nowhere and took Daphne's arm. A little too firmly for comfort. "For goodness sake, what is this nonsense about the champagne? Most of us have had at least a sip and now you're frightening people." She steered Daphne to the door leading to the kitchen. "Let's find Zeke but I want to know what this is about!"

Ilona was right behind and trying to calm everyone. "Just a slight hiccup! Champagne might be old…flat? Anyway, we'll arrange some fresh glasses so keep on enjoying the lovely food."

Unless it was the food!

Daphne tried to turn back but Tracy wasn't letting go and before she knew it, they were in the hallway.

"Right. What is going on?" Tracy released Daphne.

"Amanda has collapsed. Near the restrooms."

"Is that all?" Tracy rolled her eyes. "She's been getting stuck into the drinks since before the ceremony. Told you she likes her alcohol."

"No. No, she is in a bad way. Just like Petra, but Fred asked me to find Zeke as he has medical training."

Ilona hurried past to the kitchen, and returned almost straight away. "He isn't there. Nobody is."

"I'll call him." Tracy dialled.

A phone began to ring. Daphne followed the sound to the door she'd opened earlier. The one to the room with the embalming equipment and chemicals.

"Let me see!" Tracy pushed past Daphne and flung the door open. "Noooo!"

Zeke lay on the floor, phone in his hand and his eyes staring at the ceiling.

A TERRIBLE DAY

Daphne was right behind Tracy. It took a moment to process the scene in front of her. Zeke was lifeless. His skin was red and tiny beads of sweat peppered his forehead. His phone was in his palm. A champagne glass was shattered near the corner and a couple of plastic containers had fallen from the shelf. Had he grabbed at it to stop himself falling?

"Zeke. Zeke. No, no, no, no." Tracy moaned. She sat on the floor at his side and ever so gently closed his eyelids. "Not little Zeke."

"He's her nephew," Ilona whispered. "This can't be happening."

But it was.

Daphne found herself in the hallway, leaning against the wall rapidly blinking her eyes. The thudding of her heart filled her ears and her legs were like pillars of unmoveable concrete.

People ran down the hallway and piled into the room.

Cries.

Movement in and out.

Someone arrived with a first aid kit and Daphne let out a sob at the futility.

Poor Zeke was gone but what about Amanda?

Legs working again, Daphne retraced her steps. The reception room was in chaos. People were forcing their way through a bottleneck at the door. Desmond watched them from near the podium, still holding the glass of champagne.

"Is it true?" he asked.

Daphne had no chance of getting to Amanda until the door was clear. "Why don't you put that down. I am worried there's something wrong with it."

"Do you believe it is poisoned?"

"Um, no. Maybe. I don't know. But surely best to be cautious?"

He held it up again to peer at the contents. "How would one know? It looks like the cheap excuse of sparkling wine it is. Smells it. Almost everybody attending took at least a sip during a speech a few minutes ago."

"Who gave the speech?"

"Sonia."

Well, that was a surprise.

Desmond waddled to a side table and placed his glass on it. "She thanked us all for coming here. Said her mother would have been touched. And encouraged us all to collect our gifts before we left. It always takes her a bit of time to adjust to changes and she's doing better today."

"Do you know where Sonia is?" Daphne asked.

"She left as soon as she stopped talking. It was a bit odd. When she took off earlier, it was through the main door but she came back through the service door."

The opposite way Fred went earlier.

"Was Tracy with her?"

Desmond shook his head and his heavy jowls wobbled. "Tracy has a way of sneaking around so nobody knows where she's come from. She followed Sonia out. Then when you began banging on about the champagne, there she was again. Quite a talent."

Sonia and Tracy had left the area near the restrooms but Daphne had been between them and the main door. If Sonia returned through the service door, then there had to be another way through and she must have passed the room where Zeke was. Had he already been deceased? Or had she heard noises come from behind the closed door and kept going? Or had she killed him?

Get a grip, Daph. That's silly.

"I have to go and check on Amanda." She said.

"What's wrong with Amanda?"

"We were talking and she lost consciousness. Like Petra."

The doorway was clear now. Why had everyone been so quick to leave? Unless they thought it was dangerous here. Perhaps it was. Perhaps the champagne had nothing to do with this and something in the food, or the environment did.

A siren wailed in the distance.

Desmond headed towards the service door and Daphne went in the other direction. A handful of people lingered out here and they stared at her as she rushed past. Along the hallway.

Fred stood with Daphne's jacket looped over his arm and his eyes focused on the floor where Amanda lay.

His own jacket was over her head and shoulders.

Daphne covered her mouth with a hand as the enormity of this struck her.

Murdered.

Three people murdered.

What else could it be?

John parked a bit down the road from the funeral home. There were cars on both sides of the street and people congregated on the grassy area out the front. Adam was already here. The benefits of lights and a siren. He'd driven into the circular driveway and run into the funeral home.

An ambulance turned in and stopped behind the patrol car. Someone was there to meet it. One of the pallbearers from the funeral who worked for Fred. The man waved his arms around as the paramedics unpacked medical bags. He was agitated as he addressed them. "You're too late."

Alarming words. John sprinted.

Inside, the place was almost deserted. No staff to be seen and no Daphne. He was about to phone her when she came around a corner, head down and feet dragging.

"Daphne! You look so upset." He held his arms open and the minute she was close enough, he wrapped her up in them. "Oh, you're shaking. Tell me what happened to Amanda. You said she collapsed like Petra. The paramedics are here."

She mumbled something against his chest.

The paramedics followed the staff member in the direction Daphne had come from.

"See, they're here now."

Daphne pulled back so he was able to see her face. His heart dropped at the sadness in her eyes. "Too late, love. Too late for them both."

"Both?"

"We found Zeke as well. He was already gone."

"Let's go." He took her hand but she didn't move.

"I can't, John. I was with Amanda when she collapsed so there will be questions. And people need comfort."

"Which people?"

"Tracy for one." Now, her eyes glistened and he squeezed her hand. "Zeke was her nephew and she found him."

This was hard to take in. Three people in two days collapsing and dying in one tiny town. All associated with one funeral that went horribly wrong. Was there some illness spreading through the place? Or was it...

"Daphne. I think we should go outside and wait for Adam. This may be a crime scene."

To his relief, she nodded and let him lead her through the front door. Rather than join the other people, he found a bench not far from the entrance under a tree. For a few minutes they sat without speaking, Daphne gripping his hand.

The other police officer—Porter—arrived and instead of going into the funeral home, mingled with the people on the grass. Daphne paid her particular attention.

Why so interested, Daph?

People then began to leave the grounds. When they were all on their way, Porter headed to them and squatted in front of Daphne.

"You've had a bit of a shock, Mrs Jones. I'm Constable Porter. Beth. Everyone calls me Porter though. Adam let me know what happened and said I should ask if you can stay a little while longer. He wouldn't mind a word."

Daphne licked her lips. "We'll sit here."

"Thanks. I'll pop inside and see what's what." Beth straightened. "You should have some water. Try to relax."

Once Beth was out of sight, Daphne reached in her briefcase. "I will have some water. But relaxing is out of the question." She took a long drink then replaced the cap. "We need to be careful."

"Careful?"

She hesitated.

"Daph, I'm worried. I don't even know what happened in there or what you saw, so please, please talk to me." He turned to face her and touched her cheek with his spare hand. "You are my sweetheart and I hurt seeing you upset."

She leaned in to his touch and released a sigh. "I'm reconsidering this new lifestyle of ours. We seem to get ourselves into some dangerous situations."

"I'm listening."

"Certain comments today have been startling. Some about Edwina and her so-called secret sauce. Amanda suggested she is already buried somewhere else. Petra apparently gave her blackmail book to one of the local police and they have been using it for their own means. And I saw Zeke and Amanda kissing before the wake."

Unsure what to comment on first, John chose none of the above. Instead, he shuffled closer to Daphne and put an arm around her shoulders.

"You know what? There's plenty of time to fill me in later. Close your eyes for a few minutes and I'll let you know when Adam arrives."

As Daphne settled against him, John longed to get her back to Bluebell and be on their way. This wasn't the first time they'd come across tragedy and crime, but if he had his way, it would be the last. No more risk for his girl.

A little after seven, John set the table and invited Daphne to join him for a candlelit dinner in Bluebell. Going out tonight was a bit too much. It was great that both John and the restaurant were so flexible about changing to takeaway.

She'd had a shower after they got back half an hour ago while John went into town to collect their meal and she'd let the refreshing water wash away the worst of the feelings. For a few minutes she'd played with a treasured gift they travelled with, a snow globe depicting Rivers End, a reminder of the power of love, family, and home. Now, all she wanted was to sit with her husband and fill him in on what he didn't know.

"Ready?" he called.

"Almost." She gazed in the mirror as she brushed her damp curls. The warm evening air would dry them soon enough and she'd worry about straightening her hair tomorrow. She'd changed into loose pants and top. Perhaps they'd take a walk before dark and all she'd need to add would be some walking shoes.

"Oh, love, this looks just like a restaurant!" She gave John a kiss on his cheek as he opened a bottle of wine. "Tablecloth and nice cutlery and that lovely candle from Christie's beauty salon."

Their friend Christie had a line of scented candles, including the one on the table. 'Jasmine Sea' had special meaning to Christie and her husband, Martin, and brought the heady scent of the sea, mixed with a touch of jasmine, into the caravan.

"Please, take a seat and I'll pour us both a glass. I trust the white is to the lady's taste?" John poured with a flourish and Daphne giggled. He had a way of making everything special and just a little bit humorous and the latter was well and truly welcome. Wine poured, he served entrees kept warm in the little oven and joined her at the table.

"How lovely. I am sorry about not wanting to dine out as planned."

"I would have been more surprised if you had after such an afternoon." John picked up his glass. "To happier days."

"I'll drink to that!"

They ate their entrees and moved onto mains.

"This is delicious." Daphne swallowed her first mouthful. "The combo of goat's cheese and caramelised onion tart is yummy but the little chutney on the side makes it sensational. I wonder who made it."

"The meal?"

"Chutney. Whether it's one sold through Edwina's shop. Or a winner at the agricultural show. I'm beginning to wonder if the murders are connected by the club. The Rural Cooking, Crafting, Creating one."

John was about to take a bite but put it down. "Did you say murders?"

"I did. And I think it high time someone began investigating before anyone else falls victim to the Shady Bend killer."

BUT, WHY?

Daphne enjoyed her meal and waited until John finished his and poured them both a second glass of wine. Giving him indigestion wasn't her intention and she'd needed to think for a while.

"Spill your thoughts, Daph." John leaned back in his seat. "Tell me why you think there's a killer about."

"This town is filled with secrets and not just about the recipe of a sauce which everyone wants to get their hands on. Take Petra for example. She not only was known for keeping track of other people's personal affairs, but she wrote them down in a little book. Amanda was quite cutting about it."

"When did Amanda tell you this?"

"A few minutes before she collapsed. Said Petra gave it to someone a couple of weeks ago."

"Did she say who has it?" John asked.

"That's one of my worries, love. One of the police here have it. Might be Beth Porter or else Adam. But she claims whoever has it is using it for their own means. Blackmail, presumably."

John's mouth dropped open.

"You'll catch flies like that." Daphne observed.

Now you sound like your mother.

"You think one of the police is blackmailing people? That's a big accusation."

"Amanda's accusation, not mine. But it made me think of something Tracy said this morning. About Adam."

John nodded. "I remember. She said he's corrupt, or words to that effect. I don't believe it for a minute."

Which reminded Daphne. "When I phoned from the funeral home, you spoke to Adam. Said you were with him. But why?"

"Let me top that glass up." John opened the bottle. His face had reddened and he was intent on what he was doing. Not on her question.

"John?"

"Hm? Oh. Adam. I went to the cemetery earlier to finish what I was doing the day of the funeral. Ran into him on the way back. And we had a nice chat about Shady Bend. Want a guess at who his daughter is?"

Nice deflection, John Jones.

"His daughter? He must be fifty something at a guess. Could be anyone in their late teens to late twenties, give or take. Can I have another clue?"

"Nope. You're the sleuth." He grinned.

Daughter of Adam. Warm brown eyes.

"Constance?"

John clapped.

"She has his eyes. Interesting. So, she works for Edwina. Worked for Edwina. Now for Sonia, presumably. And Constance has custody of the last bottles of the secret sauce." She tapped the table with her fingernails as she took a sip of wine. More pieces of the puzzle. "There was talk that Edwina didn't make her own goods. And Petra was involved in some kind of competition to see if it was true.

Not to mention Petra's way of keeping tabs on people's behaviour."

"Assuming Petra was murdered, you think there's motive because of the book?" John asked.

"Perhaps. But she'd hardly give the book to Adam, whose daughter works for Edwina. I'd love to know where Beth Porter fits in."

Daphne's phone beeped a message. "Sorry. Better check this."

It was from Tracy.

Can you come to the pavilion now? Need to speak with you and I'm busy judging.

"Huh?"

"What is it?" John asked. Daphne showed him the message. "You said she's Zeke's aunt and he just passed away and she's at the show?"

Daphne typed back.

Sorry, unable to come out tonight. Happy to text or speak on the phone.

"I admit I'm a bit curious." John said.

"Me too, but we're not going back to that place."

He hadn't asked her why she'd been so distressed there but she suspected he knew something out of the ordinary had affected her.

Her phone rang.

"Guess she does need to speak to me!" Daphne accepted the call. "Hello, Tracy, I've popped you onto speaker and John is here with me."

There was a lot of background noise. Music. The mutter of a crowd.

"Would have been easier to speak face to face, but this will have to do." Tracy said.

John covered his mouth to hide a smile but the crinkling around his eyes gave it away. Tracy had such a sense of entitlement. Expecting people she'd only met a day ago to change their own plans, drive to another town, pay entry to a show they'd already been to, and find her.

"We've both had some wine, so it wasn't a good idea to drive." Daphne had no idea why she was defending her decision. "We are so sorry about Zeke. Such a dreadful thing to happen."

"It is terribly sad, isn't it? Part of life. Birth, death and so on. Anyway. Sonia got a bit carried away after her impromptu speech earlier and has decided she wants to memorialise Edwina's passing with photos of the people who helped her go to her final resting place." She snorted. "Her mystery resting place."

Daphne had no idea where this was leading and eyed her glass of wine. She had a feeling she'd need it after this.

"Can you be at Edwina's house tomorrow, please? If you can wear what you did at the funeral." Tracy said.

"Oh. Um, I guess I can. Who else will be there?" Daphne asked.

There was a sigh. An exasperated one. "I told you already. The people who helped. Pallbearers, apart from Zeke and Pet. Naturally. Fred. Ilona, I suppose. If you come along, you'll see."

John nodded across the table. He wasn't smiling now, just listening intently.

"What time? And can you send me the address please?"

"I'd say ten. Will text you later with the details. Gotta go because these scones won't judge themselves and I've taken up more time away from judging than I should."

With that, Tracy hung up.

Daphne reached for her glass.

After a special treat of strawberries and cream, Daphne opened her notebook while John logged onto his laptop. He uploaded some photos from his phone.

"I have nothing for your website. I know you prefer to show happy photos on there, but sometimes people need to see some of the more sombre moments. Gives them a sense of confidence in your kindness and care at such a difficult time." John said.

She didn't feel very kind or caring. Just a bit numb.

"I'm not sure about photos of a funeral. Although I do agree potential clients need to see what a funeral might look like with me officiating. This is a part of what I do but after this week…" She bit her lip.

"After this week?"

"I'm giving strong consideration to following Ilona's lead and keeping to happy celebrations. Not at all certain I have what it takes to do more funerals and goodbyes." Daphne wasn't a quitter. If anything, she took setbacks as a challenge. But lately she'd seen the worst of people and it was getting to her.

He patted her hand. "If you decide to restrict your services then I'll support your decision. Nothing matters more than your mental and physical health, so take your time, but know I've got your back."

"I love you, John Jones."

"And I love you. Are you up to going to this photo thing of Sonia's?" John asked as he closed the laptop. "Bit of an odd request."

"Bit of an odd person, is Sonia." Daphne said. "As is Tracy. And Desmond. I wonder what their relationship looks like on a day-to-day basis. Sonia takes photographs and sells them as postcards. And lives in a cottage on her mother's property."

Daphne started a new page in her notebook. "I suppose

I'll need to tell Adam, but I'd forgotten about something I heard earlier. Sonia was upset because Tracy made a big deal about the secret sauce when she spoke at the wake. How she expected to be the recipient of the recipe and had big plans for it. Anyway, Sonia called her out claiming Tracy put her at risk because Desmond and Fred would be breathing down her neck trying to get it first."

John frowned and he leaned forward. "At risk? I wonder what kind of risk?"

"No idea."

Daphne wrote some notes based on what she'd just told John. Then added a subheading.

Who wants the sauce and why?

"Well, as interesting as this is, nobody knows if those poor people were murder victims. There may be a logical explanation which has nothing to do with the recipe, or the blackmail book." John said.

"At the funeral home, Adam mentioned there are homicide detectives arriving in the morning. And that the funeral home was off limits to everyone, including Fred, until the detectives made a call on it. The police are treating this like murder."

Under the subheading, Daphne wrote a few lines.

1. *Tracy. Intends to commercialise sauce.*
2. *Desmond. Unknown reason.*
3. *Fred. Possibly thinks he has a right, being Edwina's ex.*
4. *Constance. Because she loves the sauce.*

"You know, Sonia didn't say if she had the recipe or not. Just that it was nobody else's business what she knew. One has to wonder how long this sauce had been the object of so many people's interest." Daphne said.

"Interest or greed? Sounds as if more than one person

believed this sauce has the potential to make them money." John glanced through the window. "Still light enough for a walk. Do us good to take a stroll."

Although Daphne preferred to stay right where she was, John was right. Keys and phones collected, they set out in the direction of the back of the camping park.

"I noticed a path through the trees earlier." John pointed. "There's meant to be a stream around here so shall we take a look?"

"I'm sorry you've not got any fishing in, love." Daphne looped her arm through his. "I bet you're looking forward to the conference weekend."

He grinned. "Access to one of the best fishing river's in the state? I am!"

"Still can't believe they invited me." It lifted Daphne's spirits remembering her invitation to the annual Celebrant's Conference next month. It was a weekend at an exclusive resort in the high country with fifty like-minded people and lots of interesting speakers. John was joining a few other spouses for an overnight camping trip fishing. "I might need to walk more and eat less so I can fit into that polka dot dress again."

"Or you could get it adjusted."

Nice thought. Daphne touched her stomach which was too rounded for her liking. No, she'd work on dropping a little weight. Best to care for one's health.

They turned onto the path, which was wide and firm underfoot and wound through pretty bushland. Native flowers abounded and an echidna ambled across without bothering to look at them, John quickly snapped some photos before it vanished again. After a few minutes, bushland gave way to a little village with a handful of houses and one general store.

"Well, I had no idea this was here!" Daphne said. "Such a cute, peaceful spot."

A park was ahead with a pond and gazebo. And in the gazebo, two people were embroiled in a heated argument.

So much for peaceful.

Their voices carried and Daphne gasped. "Ilona and Desmond."

"We should go." John said.

"No. In case it gets out of hand."

"I still cannot believe you think Edie would want you to buy her property!" Ilona sounded furious. "She's always maintained Sonia was to have the two cottages and land. And for the shop to go to—"

"Then she should have made a will." Desmond snarled. He leaned on a walking stick and even from this distance, his face was beet red.

To Daphne's surprise, John led them both closer, keeping to the tree line.

"Well, what if she did? You all assume she didn't. You and Fred and Sonia. Just because there's nothing lodged with a solicitor doesn't mean there's no will. She knew her health was deteriorating and she worried about the future. She also knew you lot would all swoop like vultures so don't be surprised if there is a will." Ilona put her hands on her hips.

"You are bluffing. I have every right to that piece of land and you know it."

"What is he talking about?" John whispered.

"Tell that to Sonia." Ilona said.

"I will. Time she knew the truth. Time everyone knew the truth." Turning his back on Ilona, Desmond stepped down onto the grass.

"Wait!" Ilona flew down to get in front of him. "Sonia won't cope. At least let her get through tomorrow and then we can have a proper meeting. You, Sonia, Fred. Me. Even

Tracy if she insists. But we can work through this. Please, Desmond."

"Very well. She can have her photo session and I'll play nice. But sooner or later Edwina's body will turn up and when it does, my bet is it'll prove she didn't have a heart attack. At least, not without some help."

He lumbered away, barely using the walking stick.

Ilona was open mouthed.

Daphne made a move to go to her but John held her arm and nodded in Ilona's direction.

She took out a phone and dialled. "We have a problem. A big, oafish problem."

STAY OR GO?

"The last thing I want to do is worry you. But Desmond is set on telling the world what he believes about Sonia and she'll be the one hurt by it all." Ilona continued.

Daphne and John tip toed their way closer.

"I don't know how to stop him, but he did agree to leave his big announcement until after her session tomorrow. And I want you there. If truth is coming out then you need to be part of it."

Ilona sank onto the bench and listened to the person on the other end of the phone.

Although John had no time for gossip and even less for inflammatory conversation, there was something going on here which he couldn't ignore. People dying. Talk about blackmail and corruption. And secrets everywhere. He had every intention of leaving with Daphne after the photo session tomorrow but until then, wasn't about to turn his back on what might be important information.

Listen to yourself!

He shook his head. Too much time hanging around with Daphne.

"Okay?" Daphne whispered.

Hanging around with Daphne was the best part of his life. "Shh. Listen."

From their position it was impossible to see Ilona's face, as she was side-on to them and in the shadow of a tree. A shadow being just one of many creeping across the grass as the sun closed in on the horizon. Darkness would fall within minutes.

"What worries me, sweetie, is what will happen if Desmond—or any of the others—puts more pressure on Sonia to hand over the recipe. She's trying hard to be brave but I see her pain and the last thing we want is for her to fall apart because of this. Her state of mind is fragile at the best of times and these are far from the best of times."

Ilona's head bobbed up and down in agreement to whatever was said in return.

"Stay strong. The truth will come out but until Edwina is located, I think we have to protect what is important. Let's talk in the morning."

Ilona hung up the call. She got to her feet and left the park without so much as a glance behind.

"Well, well, well." Daphne said. "What do you make of that?"

"Let's head home as we talk. Didn't think to bring a flashlight."

"I wonder who Ilona was speaking with? She called them 'sweetie', so someone she's close to?" Daphne asked.

"Some people use endearments for everyone but I've not noticed Ilona doing it. We know who it wasn't. Sonia or Desmond. And who are the 'others' she referred to? Who would pressure Sonia to release her mother's secret recipe, I wonder?"

"All good questions." Daphne took her phone out. "I might turn on the flashlight function because this path is dark." A sudden shaft of light appeared from her phone. "Much better. Where were we? Oh, the others. What we know is that a few people have either expressed an interest in getting it, or a third party has mentioned them."

"Tracy."

"Yes. She jumped straight into my mind. That woman is quite open about wanting to get her hands on it and commercialise the sauce. Why she believes she has any right to it though is a mystery because she comes across as having a real sense of entitlement about it, yet she wasn't close to Edwina." Daphne waved the phone around, and a pair of startled eyes stared back from the undergrowth.

"A wallaby." John observed. "Who else. Fred?"

"Definite maybe. He was married to Edwina although I don't know when. But he may believe he has a right to whatever she created. What doesn't make sense is why he'd try to take it from Sonia. Whether he is her father or not, he was married to her mother. She has priority."

It was a mystery. Not enough facts and far too many snippets of unverified information.

The path curved in the direction of the camping park, the drone of generators filling the air. He would have to pick up some more fuel for theirs tomorrow if they stayed another night. Hopefully, they'd be on their way once Daphne attended the photo session. He'd have suggested giving it a miss but Daphne wasn't one to let people down.

Be honest, John. You're curious about Edwina's property.

To see the place with his own eyes, rather than through a photograph, held a lot of appeal. He might ask Sonia if he might photograph some of the garden.

"Oh. Is that Adam?"

They were in sight of Bluebell. A patrol car was parked behind John and Daphne's car and the interior light was on.

"Looks like it." With a touch of frustration at yet another

interruption when Daphne needed a chance to relax, John took her hand. "Let's see why he's here."

"I had no intention of bothering you both tonight." Adam followed Daphne inside Bluebell with John climbing in last and closing the door. "I'll be as quick as I can."

"Sit yourself down and I'll get you a coffee. Or would tea be more to your liking?" Daphne asked, already filling the kettle.

"That's too generous of you."

"You look exhausted. Have you had dinner?" Daphne frowned. She'd not got to making cookies yet. It would have to be store bought.

John motioned for Adam to sit and with a thankful smile, the officer did.

"I just finished a burger while I waited. Coffee sounds wonderful."

Daphne made three coffees while John and Adam chatted about the weather. Warm days were forecast with the possibility of a storm tomorrow night. Best be at the next town by then. She placed the coffees down and a plate of the biscuits, then slid beside John.

"Thank you for this." Adam wrapped his hands around the cup. "Just sitting here for a few minutes is nice." He glanced around. "What a pretty caravan you have."

"We love her. Bluebell." John said with a grin. "Took me a while to get used to towing, but now it feels weird if she's not behind the car."

Daphne blew on her coffee. Why was Adam here? Earlier, when he'd come to talk to her at the bench outside the funeral home, the conversation was brief. He'd asked her a handful of questions about Amanda and Zeke, apologised for keeping her waiting, and left. There'd been no mention of follow up questions or them staying any longer. Of course, he'd had a lot to deal with. A second ambulance arriving. Two bodies removed—from a funeral home of all places. And more patrol cars as out of town police arrived to help set a perimeter around the property.

"This is nice coffee, Daphne." Adam said. "And I do apologise for just dropping in so late."

"How long were you waiting?" John asked.

"Only long enough to eat my burger. I figured you'd gone for a walk seeing as your car was still here. Thought I'd eat and if you hadn't returned, I'd leave a note."

"So, to what do we owe the pleasure of your company?" Daphne offered a small smile but her heart was pitter-pattering too fast. She'd almost reached a sense of acceptance of the events of the afternoon, even with overhearing the odd conversations at the park, but something told her the news ahead wasn't pleasant.

Adam sighed. "I have some news. Preliminary results on Petra West's toxicology screen show levels of a poison. An unusual one related to cyanide."

"Cyanide!" Daphne gasped. "But the symptoms weren't the same. No sudden death after foaming at the mouth…oh, that's more like something from a movie."

Adam grinned. "Very much like a movie. This appears to have a natural source. She ingested something containing enough of the compound to be fatal but there is ongoing testing to identify what that something is."

"Champagne."

"We don't know. And there's not sufficient evidence to point towards this being a deliberate act. Which brings me to Amanda and Zeke." Adam said.

His face was drawn with sadness. He'd known these people and may have been close to some of them, for all

Daphne knew. It tugged at her. Even if she hadn't decided yet if he was involved.

"You were with Amanda when she fell ill. I understand this is difficult, but would you mind running through those moments again. Earlier, I had a million things going on and want to be certain of your observations. I might write this down." He took out his notepad.

Daphne did her best to remember every detail as she recounted the awful minutes around Amanda's collapse. How she said her stomach hurt. And appeared lightheaded. Her flushed skin. Her final words to Daphne.

"She did something wrong?" Adam repeated. "Nothing else?"

"Nothing else. And then Fred arrived and told me to find Zeke. That he had medical training."

"You mentioned Amanda suggesting Edwina is already buried. There's just no evidence, not from our preliminary investigation, supporting her being removed from the funeral home."

"When the casket fell, Zeke had a quick look through the crack where the lid opened. He was dumbfounded. And I do mean that. He looked straight at me with a look of confusion and said the casket was empty." Daphne said.

"Yes, I spoke to him at length and he was shocked about it. I have no doubt he knew nothing about Edwina's disappearance."

She pushed her cup away, undrunk. "What about Fred? Did he suspect Zeke of having anything to do with moving the body?"

"Doubt Zeke, or any of the other staff for that matter, had the chance to move it. Fred insisted on managing every aspect of Edwina's time at the funeral home. They were married for a long time and he felt it was the one thing he could do for her to maintain her dignity and pay his own respects. Zeke is actually the only one who saw Edwina there."

"But Zeke did confirm he saw her?"

"Yes. And he helped collect her that nigh." Adam flashed a sudden smile. "No need to imagine Fred with a shovel in her garden. And you must remember there was a doctor's certificate signed so her remains definitely went to the funeral home."

Fragments of conversations played on Daphne's mind. Now wasn't the time to consider them. She needed a quiet caravan and her notebook.

"Adam, what is being done to ensure nobody else gets ill?" John asked. "I ask because a lot of people were at the wake."

"Nobody else has reported any signs of illness, thank goodness. If, and it is a big if, it was the champagne, then it might have been restricted to one bottle. The contaminant appears to only have been ingested by Amanda and Zeke which suggests they unfortunately drank from the same bottle."

"But…Petra." Daphne said.

Adam's shoulders slumped. "I know. And this is the problem. We don't have a conclusive answer to what we're looking for. A forensics unit will arrive first thing tomorrow and that will help. I have officers watching the funeral home tonight to make sure nobody goes in. All the champagne bottles were moved to a storeroom and are locked inside, along with glasses and anything else the team thought needed attention."

"You did remove the jam?" Daphne asked as a thought struck her.

"Jam?"

"The rhubarb and apricot jam from the other day." She reminded Adam.

"You know, we couldn't find any at all in the funeral

home and Fred had no idea about it. None of the staff did. I wonder if Petra was confused with another variety?"

How would someone who makes jam ever confuse the flavours? Something wasn't right here. Did Petra take the jar home, perhaps? Perhaps someone should check her house.

"Do you think it was intentional? I mean, is there a reason anyone would target those three people in particular?" Daphne might not see the connection but Adam, with his knowledge of the town, would have to have an opinion on it.

He shook his head. "Been trying to work it out for hours. Petra had some character traits which made her unpopular at times, but I can't see anyone killing her over them. Amanda hadn't been part of the 'in' group in ages. How Zeke fits in I have no idea."

But I do.

"Er…did you know they had something, um, going on?"

"Going on?"

Daphne filled him in on how she'd accidentally come across Amanda and Zeke in the kitchen.

"Now I've heard everything." Adam said. "Why anything surprises me in this town—anyway, I've taken up enough of your time." He stood. "You've been very helpful. Again."

"We met your beautiful daughter today." Daphne said.

The lines of tiredness on Adam's face disappeared as his eyes lit up.

"Did you go to the shop?"

"We did." John opened the door. "Came home with a bag of delightful wares and the taste of many samples on our lips."

"Connie likes looking after her customers. And she loves that shop. Glad you met her." He stepped down and Daphne and John joined him. "Be a pity if Sonia sells. For both of them, really."

A moment later he was driving away, waving through the

window as the patrol car nosed along the dirt road. Daphne stared after him.

"Coming in, doll?"

"I wonder what he meant."

"Meant about what?" John held the door for Daphne.

"About it being a pity for both Constance and for Sonia if the shop is sold. Do you think he just meant it would be sad to see Edwina's shop go?" Daphne made it inside and collected the coffee cups as John locked the door.

"Well, what else would he mean?"

That there might be a fourth death in town if his daughter risked losing her beloved job? That with Sonia out of the way, Constance might have a shot at keeping it?

"Nothing, dear. Nothing at all."

CLUES AND SECRETS

John was up early and snuck out of Bluebell. He waited near the door for a minute, listening. Hoping he'd not disturbed Daph.

The air was warm. Humid. No wonder there was a forecast of a storm later. With a bit of luck, they'd be in Benalla and the storm wouldn't follow. He knew Daphne tried to be brave but had never overcome her fear of thunder. There'd been one time she'd pushed all those feelings aside. A stormy night in Rivers End. Christie was lost at sea and a rescue was underway on the beach. Along with many of the townsfolk, Daphne had braved the terrible conditions to set up a station complete with medical supplies, food, water, and lots of blankets. He'd rarely been prouder of her than on that night.

With a shake of his head to dispel the rather gloomy thoughts, John followed the path they'd taken last night. It was light enough to walk without a flashlight and John took his time, hoping to come across more of the wildlife. But he made it all the way to the park before he saw anything worth photographing.

A fine mist rose from the pond. Through the trees, the

first rays of light transformed the mist into hovering gold droplets and John hurried to capture the gorgeous image before it disappeared. All too quickly the mist evaporated, leaving a family of ducks in charge of the water.

He wandered to the gazebo and perched on a seat to see what he'd got, smiling at the crystal-clear photographs. These were as good as he'd ever shot.

The gazebo was large enough for a dozen or so people to sit or mingle, with a high, curved roof and open sides, two steps up from the ground. At the side of the steps was a board with information about the region and John stopped to read.

In the middle was an illustrated map covering Shady Bend, this town, and two others in close proximity. Walking paths were highlighted and interesting spots indicated.

"Shady Gorge. Windy Orchard Peak…sounds unsuitable for growing fruit." He traced a path to another town which had different shops highlighted. "Fresh produce. Herbs and flowers. Timber furniture…wait on." John peered closer. "Alfie's Timber Creations. Alfie."

He stepped back and took a photo of the board. Then scratched his head. Thanks to the panicked phone call from Daphne yesterday, he'd had no chance to ask Adam about anything other than his finding in the cemetery.

"I noticed a headstone for Moira Browne." He'd said when he caught up with Adam at the police station.

The other man's smile had dropped. "We lost her when Connie was a young child. Still miss her every day."

And then the phone rang and he'd not had the opportunity to ask if Adam was related to an Alfred Browne. He needed to ask someone or for that matter, visit the shop himself. Just not with Daphne.

John glanced at the lightening sky and left the gazebo.

There had to be a way to see for himself. If he left Daphne at Edwina's then he'd have time.

Had he found her father? His step was lighter than usual. If locating Alfred Browne came from their detour to Shady Bend, then some of the distress of the past few days was worth it. As long as Alfred wanted to see Daphne, of course.

One problem at a time.

A few minutes before ten, John parked outside the address Tracy had messaged to Daphne. There were no other cars in sight. And no people.

"We're a bit early, John. I'm happy to wait for one of the others to arrive if you want to go exploring."

"Are you sure? I don't mind waiting with you."

Ever since John had arrived back at Bluebell this morning, he'd been distracted. He'd mentioned some peak or orchard or something and said how much he'd enjoy taking some photos. Which struck Daphne as odd after he'd been so keen to visit Edwina's place.

"No, you go take photos and there might still be time for you to take some here." She climbed out and leaned back in to give him a kiss. "Have fun."

She watched him drive away until the street was quiet. In fact, there was no sign of any movement anywhere along here. Admittedly it was more of a country lane than a street, with wide, overgrown grass verges in place of footpaths and only a handful of cottages set back from their gates. Very pretty in its own way. There was no shelter out here though and the temperature was climbing. If she went up the driveway, she could stand beneath a rather imposing oak tree and wait.

A glance at her watch told she had a few minutes before

the starting time so she picked up her soft briefcase and stepped through the open gate. Made of timber, the gate was old and in need of repairs, with some boards barely hanging on. It had been pushed into its open position long enough that grass had grown up through the panels.

The driveway was steep.

One step at a time, Daph.

Pity she'd not worn more sensible shoes but who'd have known there'd be a hill to climb?

She sucked in air. "Almost…there."

And then she was at the tree and took a minute to catch her breath leaning against its wide trunk.

From here the house—or cottage, rather—from the postcard, was a short distance away. Between Daphne and the cottage was one of the most beautiful gardens she'd seen. The postcard didn't do it justice.

For a moment, Daphne breathed deeply of the fresh air and allowed the country atmosphere to soak in. Grass tickled her ankles. The slightest of breezes rustled the branches above her. Far away, a cow lowed. So serene.

If John wasn't here to take photos, then she'd take some for him. Her phone camera wasn't as snazzy as his, but it wasn't a slouch either. She pointed, focused, and snapped away for a few minutes, zooming in on different garden beds, trees, or little touches. There were plenty of the latter, from stone benches with a backdrop of a weeping silver birch to tasteful ornaments peeking through colourful groundcovers.

A movement near the cottage caught her eye through the lens and after taking another shot, she lowered the phone. The front door was ajar.

Tracy had said the cottage was empty as Edwina had lived alone. Sonia's home was on the far side of the land but it might be her inside, getting things ready for the photo shoot. Which really should be starting any minute.

"Might ask Sonia if I'm too early." What if Tracy had given her the wrong time?

Daphne left the shade.

The driveway was topped with large loose pebbles making it difficult to walk in small heels, so Daphne cut across the lawn. Compared to the lower part of the property, the lawn was lush and short. How tempting to kick off her shoes and sink her toes into the soft grass.

But she ignored the temptation and made her way past a ceramic bird bath, disturbing a couple of rosellas in the midst of cleaning themselves.

The outside of the cottage was in need of some love. The metal roof was rusted on the ends overhanging a small verandah. Weatherboards—like the gate—needed new paint at the very least, with some rotted through where water stains ended. Window frames had seen better days and the windows themselves were grimy. The comparison to the immaculate and obviously loved gardens was stark. And strange.

There was no screen door, just a plain wooden door which was open about halfway. Daphne raised her hand to knock.

"Why are you here?" The words were screamed from inside. Sonia.

"Oh, I'm sorry—" Daphne took a step back.

"Are you trying to steal the recipe?" Sonia sounded furious.

"No, dear, I just—" Daphne started.

"You have no right to be in my mother's home."

But how can she see me?

"Leave now. Before I…I, phone for help." There was less conviction in Sonia's tone.

A muffled voice, a different voice, spoke. Too softly to hear the words but it was a male voice. Daphne was sure.

"Oh my very goodness, she wasn't yelling at me." Daphne whispered.

Somewhere, a door slammed. Daphne retreated, retracting her steps across the grass. No further sounds came from the cottage and by the time Daphne reached the tree, a car was pulling into the driveway. Tracy was at the wheel with passengers in the front and back.

Play it cool.

She plastered on a bright smile and followed the car to where Tracy was climbing out. "Beat us here, Daphne! Good show." She opened the back door. "Out you get, you lot."

'You lot' was Fred, and the two pallbearers who worked for Fred. And from the front seat, a woman with a camera climbed out. She barely nodded at Daphne before heading onto the lawn.

A motor scooter chugged up the incline carrying Ilona, her long black dress hitched up exposing her legs and horse-riding boots. She wore a backpack.

"Right. Now we need Desmond and Sonia." Tracy said.

"Sonia's in the cottage."

"She is?" Tracy glanced at the open front door. "You've been inside?"

Daphne shook her head. "No. I was going to knock but…" Perhaps she should be careful with her words. "Um, I heard her in there and decided not to intrude."

Tracy raised her eyebrows.

Ilona opened her backpack and swapped the boots for slip on shoes. "Can't ride with these on."

"Nobody cares about your footwear." Tracy said. "I'll round the others up."

Off she strode, up the driveway with no trouble on the pebbles.

"Despite how she talks, she's not all bad." Ilona said. She'd pulled a long sash decorated with real flowers from the backpack and was winding it around her waist. "I officiated at her wedding a few years ago and she was a different woman. Pleasant. Thoughtful. Sonia was her bridesmaid, believe it or not."

Not the Tracy of today then.

Ilona continued as she dug around for a hairbrush. "Lost her husband only a year later. Car accident—hit by a truck which then kept going. Don't think she ever forgave poor Adam for not finding the other driver. Wasn't his fault."

Daphne added this to her mental file. If Tracy felt that way about Adam it might account for her belief he was corrupt. Might be nothing to do with recent events.

"How awful for her."

"Yes. And she was in the car. So were Edie and Sonia, all on their way back from judging a show in another town." Ilona hung her head and her shoulders slumped. "Sonia had a head injury and has never really recovered. Tracy swings between silly guilt about Sonia being hurt in their car, and impatience that she hasn't got better. That night changed everybody."

Such a tragedy would be hard to move on from, injuries or not.

"I'm sure it means a lot to Tracy that you are always so kind to her."

"Oh. You are so sweet." Ilona hugged Daphne, then returned to dragging the hairbrush through her long hair, frowning as it snagged. "When are you and John leaving town?"

"We hope this afternoon, depending on whether the police want any further interviews. I have a wedding in Benalla this weekend and would love the chance to visit a hairdresser and for John to get some fishing in."

"Such a pity all of this has happened. Edie disappearing and poor Pet, and Amanda and Zeke." Ilona gave up trying to tame her hair and tossed the hairbrush away. "Any other time you'd love being in Shady Bend. Lovely food. You've been to the shop?"

Daphne couldn't help smiling. "If you mean Edwina's then yes. And we had the most wonderful tasting plate and bought a lot more than intended. Constance is so nice."

Tracy was waving at them.

"Let's hope this isn't too stressful." Ilona left her backpack under a tree beside her scooter as she and Daphne walked over to the lawn. "Constance is a darling. Sounds silly but she's a bit like a daughter to me. I'd hoped she would be here but she feels she can't close the shop again after being at the wake."

So, you were speaking with Constance last night. How interesting.

Why had Ilona wanted Constance to attend the photo session? She'd not been at the funeral. Was this concerning the shop and who would end up with ownership?

The woman with the camera was taking test shots in a couple of places. Fred's staff stood around. Fred was nowhere to be seen.

"We're missing Desmond so I've given him the hurry up on the group chat. Fred's in the cottage getting Sonia sorted." Tracy said with a glance at her watch. "Need to get a move on because I'm judging this afternoon and can't stand around here all day."

It was beside the point that she'd arrived after the arranged time but Daphne wasn't about to mention anything so provocative. Best to play nice. And hope it wouldn't be too long as the sun was beating down quite hard now. A trickle of perspiration ran down Daphne's spine. Great.

PHOTOGRAPHIC EVIDENCE

Almost ten minutes later, the front door flung all the way open and Sonia stalked out, head high. Fred followed, pulling the door closed as he left the cottage.

"Well, thank goodness. Now we just need Desmond." Tracy said as she checked her phone. "Odd. He usually replies straight away."

"Then let's begin without him." Sonia went past the small group to a lovely display of roses. "Here. This was Mum's favourite part of the garden so we'll take the photos here."

Each rose was about five feet tall, a bed of red, pink, and yellow plants. In a semi-circle around perfect lawn, they were charming. Something about them wasn't quite right though. As healthy as the ones on either end were, a couple towards the middle had drooping leaves.

"Not here, Sonia." This was Fred. He stood apart from everyone and pointed to the stone bench. "How nice to have some people sitting and others standing."

Sonia rolled her eyes, crossed her arms, and planted her feet.

The photographer returned. "This is the best spot."

Fred frowned but didn't reply. He wandered over to Daphne. "You must wish you'd never taken my original phone call."

And miss all of this?

"Goodness. It is hardly your fault this turned into such a…" Daphne clamped her lips shut to avoid saying 'mess'.

"Disaster. Tragedy upon tragedy in our small town." Fred nodded. "There's nothing more keeping you here. At least, once this final obligation is done and I want you to know I appreciate your understanding. There's some extra funds transferred to your account to compensate for all the extra time."

"Oh. Oh, well, I didn't expect that. But thank you."

An old car, spluttering as it struggled up the incline, stopped as close to the cottage as it could. The motor sounded dreadful and its exhaust dragged. The door creaked as it opened and Desmond pulled himself out using the door to support his weight. All eyes turned his way but Daphne was interested in Sonia's reaction and it was worth waiting for. The younger woman stiffened and her chin lifted.

"Sorry everyone. Took forever to get the car started. Thought I'd need to walk across."

Something about Sonia's expression told Daphne what she'd suspected. It was Desmond who'd been in the cottage before. The person who'd upset Sonia to the point of her screaming at him. Words about him not supposed to be in the cottage. And was he trying to find the recipe. The secret sauce recipe? What was it about the ingredients of a sauce which made half the people in Shady Bend act so oddly?

"If you'd have told me, I would have driven around and collected you, Desmond. Rather than hold proceedings up." Tracy moved to the middle of the rose area. "Right. Everyone, get into places. Tallest in the middle."

Daphne quickly sent John a message. "About to start.

Usual shenanigans but getting some very interesting intel. Will reveal all later!"

She muted the phone and put it away as Tracy gestured for her to stand between Ilona at the end and Desmond. Then came one of the pallbearers, Fred, Tracy, the other pallbearer, and Sonia.

"This isn't what I want!" Sonia announced.

"Just for once stop being so dramatic. We'll swap everyone around in a minute." Tracy glared at Sonia.

So did Desmond.

Talk about needing a knife to cut the tension! Ah, this reminded her. She needed to make cookies today. Why that particular thought appeared she had no idea but she knew it was long overdue to refill the cookie jar with her yummy treats. She might make two flavours.

"Daphne? You need to smile." The photographer said.

It was to commemorate someone's passing. Why smile? But Daphne did as she was asked. They all did, apart from Sonia, who looked disinterested.

"We might get individual photos now." The photographer said. "Who is first?"

Nobody moved.

"For goodness sake. Everybody exit the area. Sonia. You go first. Stand or sit or leap about but get your photo taken." Tracy was back to being bossy boots.

One by one, everyone took a turn. Ilona was last and just as she smiled at the camera, her sash fell off. Flower blossoms went everywhere and she kneeled to gather them. Several rolled onto the garden bed beneath the roses and she leaned in to collect them.

"Leave them!"

Fred was at her side in an instant.

"I'll do it. You sort out your dress."

Ilona moved to one side, fiddling with the sash. The pallbearers, photographer, and Sonia congregated near the front of the cottage. But Desmond and Tracy remained with Daphne. The other two gazed at Fred as he reached under the plants, snatching them back and avoiding touching the dirt with his hands.

"Quite right there, Fred?" Tracy asked.

"Can't have someone else's flowers contaminating these roses. Edwina would be mortified if they pick up some disease or other."

"My blossoms aren't diseased, Fred. You know I take great care of my plants." Ilona said. She tied the sash again and although there were a few empty spots, at least the bright colours stood out against her black dress. "The petals will decompose if you leave them there. Probably help them, seeing how sad those leaves are. Is nobody watering them now?"

Fred straightened with his hands full of flower heads. "I'll put these in the compost. Don't wait for me."

Before anyone had a chance to respond he disappeared between this garden bed and the next, dropping some blossoms as he went. Daphne scooped them up and followed. His behaviour interested her. The garden did as well.

She found Fred around the side of the cottage near an ornamental stone wall. He'd stopped and was gazing at it, his hands against his chest, clenching the blossoms. The wall was about three feet high, built of some light-coloured blocks of stone, and made a barrier between this part of the garden and an orchard of fruit trees.

Was this where Edwina died?

Daphne slipped behind a bush, watching through the branches so as not to disturb Fred. He'd found Edwina against a stone wall, already deceased. By his body language, this spot meant something. How awful to find her there. Even divorced, they'd apparently remained friends.

Suddenly he leaned closer to the top of the wall, peering at it. He dropped the blossoms and took a handkerchief from a pocket, wetting the corner with his tongue. Fred applied the wet patch with vigour to a small area of the stone wall, scrubbing and then muttered a curse word. He shoved the handkerchief away and grabbed the fallen flowers before stomping off and disappearing through a gate.

Grabbing her phone and somehow managing with one spare hand, Daphne zoomed in as far as she could on the spot but all she got was a blur.

She closed in on the wall, snapping photos without focusing because her hand was shaking and she struggled to walk making a call let alone get the most from a camera.

Please don't come back yet. Please don't.

Almost there. Almost.

From behind the gate, another curse.

She stopped abruptly and zoomed in to take one photo before shoving the phone away.

"What are you doing here?" Fred opened the gate.

"Ah. Wondered where you are. You dropped these back in the rose garden and I thought I should save you another trip to the compost." She held out the blossoms, which were rather worse for wear thanks to squashing them into one hand.

He gaze her a curious look. Did he believe her?

"Thanks. Here, I'll take them. You go back."

"I don't mind coming with you. Or waiting here."

"No! I mean, Sonia wanted some photos of you and her together." He took the blossoms. "Getting so hot now it can't be pleasant in your jacket. I know I'd like to take mine off. I'll catch up."

He really didn't want her here.

"Yes, it certainly is warm. And humid."

Fred went to the gate but instead of going through, stood.

With a smile, Daphne retraced her steps, glancing over her shoulder when she was on the other side of the bush. He'd gone. It wasn't worth risking being caught again. Hopefully she had one good image of whatever he'd been so interested in.

Alfie's Timber Creations was frustratingly hard to locate.

John had driven past the caravan park where they were staying, beyond the tiny town with the pond and gazebo, and followed a winding road into a valley. There was only a petrol station, the smallest supermarket he'd ever seen, and a pub along the main street. John parked and checked the photograph he'd taken of the map. It was far from exact so he did an internet search. This gave him an address and after more than a couple of wrong turns, he stopped near a yard with a shed along a narrow dirt road. Surrounded by high chain fencing, there was a faded sign on a locked gate.

Alfie's Timber Creations.

The shed was fairly large with double doors that were locked with a heavy padlock. Only the sight of a couple of hanging pots with healthy flowers restored the hope this wasn't an abandoned property.

Still, it didn't help him find answers.

He wandered the length of the fence. There were no other signs. No opening hours or contact details.

A couple of boys riding pushbikes went past then circled back.

"Not open today, mister." One of the boys pulled up, cleverly keeping balance by adjusting his weight and moving the pedals back and forth. "Tomorrow. Maybe."

"Thank you. Do you know who works there?"

"Old dude. Cranky as."

The other boy rode off.

"What's his name?" They wouldn't be here tomorrow. "Do you know where he lives."

"Somewhere up the hill. But you don't want to visit. Told you he's cranky." The boy followed his friend.

"Thanks." John did want to visit. Cranky or not, John needed to know the man's identity. But if he was Daphne's father, arriving unannounced on his doorstep was not the right way to make first contact. Talking to Adam might be the best solution.

Back at the gate, he took a couple of photographs. Perhaps he could ask Ilona. Out of all the people he'd met, only she and Adam and Constance seemed trustworthy. As long as she didn't tell Daphne until he'd had a chance to follow things up because if her hopes were raised and nothing came of it… He couldn't bear to break her heart.

"You've been through enough already."

He'd think it through. But have to think fast because Daphne was ready to leave Shady Bend and he wasn't inclined to encourage her to stay a minute longer than they needed to.

BEST LAID PLANS

"We can't leave yet." Daphne had almost thrown herself into the car when John pulled up where he'd dropped her earlier. "Let's get back to Bluebell."

He glanced up the incline. "No chance of me getting some photos, I guess?"

"Negatory. Not this time. But I took a few."

An old car rattled down the driveway and John waited until it turned onto the road before he pulled out. It went the opposite direction with Desmond behind the wheel.

"How did it go?"

Daphne kind of snorted. "Care to take any guesses?"

He smiled and accelerated. "Let me see. Tracy bossed everyone around. Sonia pouted a lot. Ilona was sweet and probably cried. Fred kept everybody on track."

"Not bad. You got the first two right. Ilona is sweet, of course, but no tears. She had some wardrobe malfunctions which kept her occupied. And Fred? He was weird." Daphne undid her jacket. "I should have taken this off."

"I can pull over."

"I'll be fine. Not far to go and then I'm changing and having a tall glass of iced tea."

The remainder of the short trip was in silence as Daphne tapped at her phone. John parked next to Bluebell and they climbed out. If anything, the temperature had risen since he'd left Alfie's and the air was dripping with humidity.

Daphne dropped her briefcase onto the seat at the table. "Be right back."

John poured glasses of iced tea and sat at the table, doing another search on his phone. This one was on the name 'Alfie Browne'. He began scrolling the list.

"Feel better already." Daphne was in looser clothes and had bare feet. She picked up her glass and sipped. "Thanks, love. Needed this. Did you get some nice photographs?"

"Photos? Oh. Not as many as I hoped for." He closed the search and put the phone on the table.

"Pity. I got a few. Some of the gardens because everyone was late and I walked up to the cottage. And overheard Sonia terribly upset with someone. Desmond. At least, I'm pretty sure."

"Pretty sure?"

"The front door was partly open and I heard Sonia yelling at someone. And the muffled voice, a man, who then left through a back door. But when Desmond arrived in his car, quite late, she wasn't happy to see him. Whoever was in the cottage, they weren't invited. She accused them of trying to steal the recipe."

"The secret sauce recipe? What is so special about it?"

"My question exactly. I have the strangest feeling this sauce of Edwina's has something to do with the unfortunate deaths." Daphne said.

"You think the sauce killed them?"

She shook her head. "Goodness me, no. But maybe their greed did. And there's more."

Daphne told John about Fred's peculiar behaviour around the rose garden and then at the stone wall.

"Did you get close enough to see what he was trying to clean?" This was a turn of events. Fred came across as a man in control of his environment. Even the disappearance of Edwina's body did little more than put him on edge.

"I tried to get photos." She opened the gallery on her phone. "I was behind a bush at first."

John chuckled.

"Well, I couldn't very well make an appearance if he was doing something suspicious. Ah, here we go." She handed the phone over.

There were lots of photos of the garden, which was even more beautiful than John imagined. He wanted to stop at each one but kept flicking through until there was one of a branch. Close up. The next few were out of focus but there was a figure in the background.

"This is good." He turned the phone to show Daphne a clear image. Fred rubbed at something on the wall with his handkerchief. Zooming in didn't reveal what though.

Another dozen images later—all random shots of grass, sky, and Daphne's feet—there was one of the wall. He pinched the screen and zoomed until it was too fuzzy, then backed out.

"Anything?"

John stood. "I'll get my laptop. Might be clearer."

"Because I have a theory."

"Keep talking." John collected the laptop from the cupboard.

"Adam said Fred found Edwina slumped against the wall. She'd had a fatal heart attack."

John connected Daphne's phone to the laptop and downloaded the images she'd taken today.

"What if it wasn't a heart attack?" she asked.

"What else would it be?"

"Maybe she fell and hit her head. And for some reason when Fred found her, he didn't notice and assumed it was her heart."

"But the doctor would have noticed. Bit hard to overlook a head injury."

Daphne tapped at the table top with her nails and her eyes had the familiar faraway look signalling she was puzzling something out.

The photos began to populate the screen and John enlarged the one he was interested in. Viewing it on the larger screen helped to a degree but it wasn't sharp enough to be certain. He'd like to go there himself and take a look. And take photos with his phone, which he'd bought mainly for the outstanding camera quality.

"John, I don't know. The way Fred was today…and Edwina's missing body. What if her death was not from natural causes, and the doctor was in on it? What if Fred killed Edwina and then he covered it up?"

He rotated the screen so she could see. "I'm beginning to think you might be onto something."

"We have to show this to the police." Daphne checked the screen for the third time. Still the same close up of the stone wall. And still the same reddish-brown splashes dried into it. "It may not be blood, but they need to make that determination."

"Would you like to go to the station?"

"I think so. Can we take the laptop?"

John nodded.

"What a dreadful turn of events if it is blood. If someone had a hand in poor Edwina's passing."

Daphne went in search of sandals. She was slipping as a sleuth. Fred was never once in her sights as a potential killer and this was all something of a shock. If her theory was right, had he been responsible for hiding Edwina's body? But why? Surely a proper burial following all the rules was the least suspicious course of action.

What is he hiding?

She pushed the thoughts aside as they drove to the police station.

Several cars, patrol and otherwise, took most of the parking in front of the station so John pulled into a spot further up the road and they walked back.

Inside, a meeting was underway. Adam, Porter, and half a dozen uniformed police stood around a whiteboard. A plain clothes officer was speaking and she stopped mid-speech when she noticed Daphne and John waiting at the counter. Adam followed her gaze and excused himself. The other officer resumed what she was saying.

"Sorry. Just in the middle of a briefing. How can I help?" Adam spoke quietly.

"Actually, we hope we can help." Daphne said. "I don't know where you are with investigating Edwina's disappearance, and this may or may not assist, but it should raise more questions. Which hopefully lead to answers."

Oh dear. That sounded complicated.

"Not sure I follow."

John set his laptop on the counter and opened it.

"I was at Edwina's cottage earlier. For a photo session with Sonia and some other people. Long story short, I followed Fred at one point and found him doing rather an odd—"

"Wait. Go back a bit. You followed Fred?" Adam's pained expression made Daphne pause and take a breath.

I've done it again.

"Well, he dropped some flowers and I tried to catch up as he had them and then I saw what he was doing and hid behind a bush and…anyway. He took out a handkerchief and tried to clean part of the stone wall."

"None of that made sense, but go ahead. What am I looking at?" he stared at the laptop screen as John showed him the original photograph of the wall. John zoomed in and suddenly, Adam was on alert. He leaned in to look better. "Can you zoom more?"

"Not without losing focus."

Adam turned. "Detective. Porter. May I borrow you both?"

The women approached and the rest of the group followed at a distance, interested, no doubt, in why there was an interruption.

"Detective Malone, this is Daphne and John Jones."

"The celebrant. You've been very helpful." Detective Malone nodded. "I understood you were leaving town today."

"Yes. Well, we still plan on that. But Daphne took a photograph this morning and we thought it best to show it to Adam." John said.

Adam repeated, more or less, what Daphne had told him apart from the muddled bits and then he, Detective Malone, and Porter huddled around the laptop. The others tried to peer over their shoulders. After a few words which Daphne couldn't make out, Adam straightened. "May we have a copy of this?"

"I'll send it to your email. Do you want all the ones Daph took today?"

"Anything you think might be of interest."

The other police returned to the whiteboard.

"We're not any further along finding Edwina. What we are working on is locating the source of the poison ingested by Petra, Zeke, and Amanda. There's no further illness, thank goodness." Adam glanced at the whiteboard. "What we know is all three consumed similar foods and drinks a short time before succumbing to the poison."

"Champagne? Jam?" Daphne asked.

Adam rolled his eyes. "Mrs Jones."

"I thought you normally call me Daphne. I just keep my eyes and ears open."

"I've emailed all of those across to you." John closed the laptop. "We shouldn't take up any more of your time."

"You've done the right thing." Adam ran a hand over his head. "Please stop hiding behind bushes though."

"I tell her the same thing." John said. "Mind you, if Daphne has a hunch, it's usually right."

I'd like to kiss you right now.

She didn't. "Adam, I think you should look at Fred more closely. I feel there's more to him than meets the eye."

"I'll visit the cottage shortly. Take one of the forensic officers up."

"Thank you." Daphne smiled at Adam. "We'll let you get back to work."

Halfway to the car, John stopped. "I left my phone on the counter. Jump in the car and I'll be right behind you." Before she could say a word, he'd gone. Wasn't like him to forget anything but it had been quite an exciting morning.

Rather than get into the heat of the car, she waited in the shade of a tree and glanced at the sky. Clear. Not a cloud. With a bit of luck, the forecast storm would fizzle out. There was enough going on in Shady Bend without adding thunder and lightning.

John was taking a while. Odd if he'd just gone to get his

phone. She was about to find him when he, and Adam, emerged from the station. They stopped just outside the door and shook hands and Adam gazed at Daphne. He lifted a hand and she waved back. Such a nice man. He couldn't possibly be corrupt but then again, sometimes the person you least suspect turns out to be the bad guy.

COOKIES AND CARDBOARD

"I'm thinking one batch of vanilla and sultanas, and one of chocolate with added choc chips." Daphne pulled two baking trays from the bottom cupboard. She had the ingredients lined up on the counter and the oven was heating, thanks to the generator going outside.

John had his head in his laptop. In fact, he'd hardly moved or said a word in the last half hour.

"And one batch with river pebbles and another with cut up pieces of paper."

Nothing.

"Tracy is going to judge them. She'll decide which one is the most delicious and then she'll want to steal my secret recipe."

"Sound delicious, doll."

It was all Daphne could do not to burst out laughing. John was so distracted she could have said almost anything. He must have realised she was looking at him for he lifted his head.

"Sorry, what did you say?"

"Would you like a pot of tea while I bake?"

He smiled. "Are you sure that's what you said? And yes, I would love that."

She filled the kettle. "What are you up to?"

"Genealogy research. That little cemetery piqued my interest about a name I saw and now I'm following a family tree." He closed the laptop. "Would you like a hand?"

"I've got everything under control. Seeing as we're staying one more night, I might as well put my time to good use. But you never really said, John. Why are we staying another night?"

After they arrived back at Bluebell, Daphne had begun packing Bluebell's interior ready for travel. Instead of going outside to do the same, as was his routine, John took Daphne's hands. "Leave it until morning, Daph. I have a feeling if we leave, we're going to have to turn around and come back."

His words weren't a complete surprise. Not when there was an unsolved case here. Several unsolved cases. Deep in her bones was the answer. Well, perhaps not in her bones, but that was how strong her commitment to finding the answers was.

John reopened the laptop. "Couple of things made me reconsider leaving today. I've had a look at the weather forecast and it seems as if the storm will miss Shady Bend but give poor Benalla a hammering. Not a fan of getting Bluebell settled at a new ground in those conditions."

"That is reason enough on its own." Daphne shook flour from the packet into a large bowl. "What else?"

"Er. Remember I ducked back to the station for my phone?"

"Yes. I waved to Adam when you both came outside again."

"Oh. Yes. Well. Anyway, he was about to go to Edwina's cottage."

"I know that, dear. Remember I was there when he said so?"

What is going on, John Jones?

"So you were. Did you say you needed a hand?"

Daphne turned around, flour on her hands and a grin on her face. "Would you mind making the tea? I seem to have messy fingers."

"Cookies?"

"Unless you'd rather wait for tea until they're cooked? Won't be too long." She could have sworn he was frowning. This was becoming a bit of a regular occurrence. Either some odd grimace or cookies disappearing when she'd known there was some left. Must be her imagination because John loved her cookies. Everyone did.

"I should enter them into the show."

John got up and reached for the teapot. "Don't do that!"

"Don't enter my cookies in the show?"

Daphne lifted her hands from the board, her heart skipping a beat. Were they really so bad?

He kissed her cheek. "Less for me if you do."

Her heart sighed. He did love them. Perhaps there was enough here to make three varieties.

Despite John's earlier enthusiasm, Daphne snuck a glance his way when he bit into the first warm cookie. He caught her looking and turned up the sides of his lips, which couldn't be easy with his mouth full. Her phone rang and she put down her own cookie before even getting a taste.

"Daphne Jones speaking."

"Daphne, it's Ilona." Her voice was both loud and stressed and Daphne held the phone away from her ear. "I'm at Petra's house and I think something is wrong here."

"Slow down a bit. Why are you at Petra's?"

"Oh. I've been tending her garden and feeding her sheep until arrangements are made. She has three sheep. One just climbed through the fence. But I think someone's been in her house and hoped you might come."

John leaned forward and Daphne put the phone onto speaker.

"Ilona, this is John. Are you in danger?"

"No. No, I don't think so. And before you ask, I have spoken to Adam and he'll be along in a bit but has his hands full. But something odd is going on. There's a parcel outside the door."

"Like a delivery?"

"Yes. It is broken. Open in one corner. And there are…jars inside."

This wasn't getting any clearer to understand.

"I know I'm not making any sense but I can show you. I mean if you would come around, I would be very grateful for your opinion." Ilona said.

"Our opinion?"

There was a long pause with only the baaing of sheep through the phone.

"Ilona?"

"I'm not sure who to trust anymore, Daphne. But I know I can trust you and John. You don't have any stakes here. Would you come and see, and tell me if I'm overreacting?"

John was nodding.

"Yes, dear. Send the address and we'll come right away."

Almost the instant she hung up, the phone dinged a message.

John was already on his feet, leaving behind the cookie with just one bite missing.

Petra West's house was the last home down a winding laneway not far from the ground where the country show was being held. From here, music and excited screams of those brave enough to try the scary rides was at odds with the occasional baaing of sheep somewhere behind the house. The garden was pretty with daisies growing through long fine grass and a collection of fruit trees scattered around.

"I'm surprised fruit does so well here." Daphne waited as John locked the car. "For some reason, Shady Bend sounds too…dark. How silly of me. It's like Edwina's property having an orchard. They are in a sheltered but sunny area and with the cold winters up here are probably in an ideal situation to thrive."

Ilona's motor scooter was parked in front of a single garage but there was no sign of her, so Daphne led the way to the front door. The parcel which concerned Ilona so much was larger than Daphne expected and looked heavy. Someone had dropped it and the cardboard corner had come apart leaving a wide gap.

"Should we look?" Daphne asked.

John didn't get a chance to answer as Ilona hurried towards them from around the corner of the house. She was in overalls and muddy boots and her hair was escaping from a ponytail.

"Sorry. I had to round her up, the sheep that is, the one who escaped and then I found I'd left the hose on and so much mud." She glanced at her boots. "But at least she's back in her paddock. I see you found the box."

A shriek of terror from some poor soul probably upside down on a ride at the show made all three of them jump.

"Have to go there this afternoon and I'm already over the noise!" Ilona said. "Anyway, this is the quandary. A box addressed to Petra which raises a whole lot of questions. Did you see inside?"

John shook his head. "If it's addressed to Petra…"

"She's not going to care at this point." Ilona pointed out. "You can see without touching. They are jars."

"Like bottling jars?" Daphne asked.

"Yes. So, what is strange about it? Petra used to be one of the most competitive makers of jams and bottled fruit in the region. For years she won just about everything and then everything changed. She still entered every so often but rarely won. As if she just didn't care anymore." Ilona nudged the box with her toe, leaving a muddy mark.

"So, you think it odd she'd have a delivery of jars?" John asked.

"A bit. But it isn't the bottles as such. Can you see the bundle on top? Here, if you slightly widen the gap," Ilona used both hands to do so, "there. Those are labels, already printed and ready to attach once the bottles are filled."

Daphne peered in but her eyesight wasn't good enough to read the label. She got her phone out and turned on the flashlight. Much better.

She gasped and stepped back.

"Daph?" John looked inside. "Does that say…no."

"Yes." Ilona put her hands on her hips. "Yes, it says *Edwina's Secret Sauces & Special Supplies.* Why. That is my question. Why would Petra be receiving jars meant for Edwina?"

There'd been speculation, accusations, about Edwina. Did she paint her own paintings? Or was it Desmond? And the jams and preserved fruit and chutneys and sauces…were the rumours true?

"Ilona, you were close to Edwina. Does this resonate with you? I've heard stories."

"About Edie not making what she put her name to?" Ilona stared off towards the show as more screams cut through the air. "Of course it resonates. I asked Edie about it one time and she said not to believe everything I hear. It wasn't a denial. Nor admission. But she'd have told me if she wanted me to know."

"You never saw any signs? Like these jars?" John asked.

Ilona turned to them. "I seek to see the best in people. Perhaps that is naïve. It may be the rumours were true but even so, it doesn't change how much I loved Edie. She was my friend, flaws and all. If Petra was working for her, then there was a good reason and with her heart condition she'd felt a sense of doom. This might all have been a contingency plan to keep income coming in for Sonia."

A patrol car pulled up outside.

"Good. I didn't want to go inside alone."

Constable Porter joined them. She glanced at the box and raised a questioning eyebrow. "Ilona, you mentioned a break in."

"I think so." Ilona pulled a key from a pocket. "Petra gave me a key when she went away so I could feed the sheep and water her indoor plants. Told me to hang on to it for future jobs." She looked at Daphne. "I do house sitting and pet walking on the side."

"And…" Porter checked her watch.

"And I can see through the window here," Ilona pointed at a vertical glass panel beside the front door, "there's a mess inside. Petra kept her place immaculate."

Everyone tried to peer through the glass at the same time, over the top of the box.

"Shall I open the door?" Ilona inserted her key. "Oh. It isn't locked."

Porter stepped up. "Let me." She turned the door handle and it opened. "You all stay here please." She unclipped her holster and stepped inside. "Police. Constable Beth Porter entering the house."

She disappeared into the house. With the door open, the

mess was apparent. A potted plant knocked over with dirt scattered across carpet. Drawers in a hallway table were open, their contents hanging out. Someone was looking for something and didn't care if they made it obvious.

Ilona looked as if she was going to follow and Daphne put a hand on her arm. "Best let the police do their job. Make sure nobody is still inside."

"I'm sure they aren't. We've been talking out here for a while so anyone in their right mind would have left through the back door. But you're right. They'll need to fingerprint the place but I just hate seeing the plant like that."

"Can we step under a tree? Bit hot out here." Daphne didn't wait for an answer. If it got any stickier, she'd melt. The other two followed, John taking out his phone. They stopped beneath a golden ash in view of the front door and John took some photos. He was getting as bad as she was. Record everything. Miss nothing.

Suspect everyone.

WHAT FRED DID

John wasn't taking random photographs. A glint in the grass caught his eye as he'd left the doorway, somewhere beyond the tree. Even zoomed in it was unclear what caused the reflection which for all he knew might be nothing more than a piece of rubbish flown over from the show. Life with Daphne taught him to record anything suspicious. Better to delete unwanted images than wish you'd taken them.

Porter was still inside the house so he wandered in the direction of the object. The grass was even longer in this part of the garden and if the sun hadn't caught it at the exact moment he'd looked the right way, he'd never have seen it.

A key.

He squatted to better see.

It was a house key on its own. Not even a loop to attach it to a keyring.

"John? Is everything alright?" Daphne was heading his way.

He straightened. "There's a house key here. I might stay with it if you don't mind letting Constable Porter know once she's out of the house."

Daphne peered into the grass. "Oh my. You are so clever finding it. Do you think whoever let themselves into the house then threw the key away? Or maybe it dropped out of their pocket or something."

"There's Porter. She's coming over."

So was Ilona. Porter was on the phone and came to a halt a few feet away as she continued a conversation. "No sign of break in. Yeah. Unlocked. Oh really? Huh, well there you go. Righto." She hung up. "What's everyone looking at?"

"Key." Daphne pointed.

Ilona moved closer. "Oh. That is one of Petra's. I'm certain."

"Interesting." Porter took some photos of her own, then slipped the key into an evidence bag. "Why does it have 'one' written on it? Any idea, Ilona?"

"Yes. She had three keys. One was hers. Two was mine. Three was hidden for emergencies. How did anyone get hold of her own house key?" Ilona teared up. "And why would someone go into her house and trash it?"

Daphne put an arm around Ilona's shoulders. "We'll get to the bottom of it, dear."

"No." Porter started back to the house. "The police will get to the bottom of it."

"And we will help them." Daphne whispered.

"I heard that." Porter called over her shoulder. "If you want to know what happened at Edwina's, you'd better catch up."

"First of all, let's set some ground rules. No repeating what I tell you. And no going into the house. Okay?"

Everyone nodded at Porter. They were all beneath

another tree closer to the house and she stood facing them, hands on her hips.

"There's a unit heading up here, including some of the forensic team who are in Shady Bend investigating other matters. Adam is busy at the station but because Desmond arrived right in the middle of it and has overheard certain information which he's already said he has no intention of keeping to himself, he says I can share what happened up at her cottage. Edwina's."

"What? What happened?" Ilona was still fragile, Daphne sensed it. Being here was clearly playing on her emotions and whatever barrier she'd erected to get her through this time was crumbling.

"Do you remember this morning, at the photo shoot, that I followed Fred with some of the flowers you lost?" Daphne asked.

"Not really. I was trying to fix the sash and then I noticed you appear from around the side of the cottage."

"Daphne noticed there was an odd mark on the stone wall." Porter said. "She took a photo and Adam and one of the forensic team were up there a bit earlier to take a better look."

"What kind of odd mark? Was it where Fred found Edwina?" Ilona's voice squeaked and Daphne grabbed her hand. "Is this about her body?"

"Not precisely. Look, at this point, Fred is at the station chatting to Adam and Detective Malone. All I can pass on is that there was some blood found on the wall. We don't know if it belongs to Edwina, but Fred has come forward and said he wasn't entirely honest about how he found her. That she had a cut on her head and he thought she'd had a heart attack and fallen against the wall. Whether she died from the heart condition or the fall we will only know if her body is recovered."

The Shadow of Daph

Tears dripped down Ilona's cheeks.

"How about you sit here in the shade." John suggested. "Do you have some water somewhere?"

Ilona sank onto the grass with a shake of her head. "I don't need water. I need Edie back and for all of this to go away." She pulled a tissue from a pocket. "I don't understand why Fred didn't say what really happened at the beginning. Why would he lie?"

Why indeed?

Rather than allow Ilona's grief to worm its way into her heart, Daphne put her mind to work. Fred had acted suspiciously at the stone wall. Now he revealed he had lied about how he found Edwina. But what would prompt such a lie? Was he afraid people might believe he'd been responsible? Or was there a reason he didn't want her cause of death investigated?

Daphne's fingers itched to get a pen and her notebook.

"No need to hang around here." Porter said. "We'll call if we have any questions."

Ilona gazed up. "I want to stay. I need to check the sheep and make sure the fence is holding where I repaired it. And what about the box?"

"The delivery? One of us can put it inside once crime scene does their thing."

"Neither Petra nor Edwina are going to use the contents." Ilona looked down at the grass and played with a blade. "Jars might as well go to Sonia."

This surprised Porter. "Sonia?"

Daphne explained about the labels.

"You think Petra was making the jams and stuff? And then putting a shop label on, which implied they were made by Edwina? Well, I never." Porter's phone beeped and she walked away.

So did Ilona's but she ignored it.

And again.

"Message, dear?"

"Just the group chat, Daphne."

All three of them looked at each other and Ilona tapped at her phone. If group chat was going, was it about Fred?

"Oh. Oh, dear, here Daphne, would you read it. I'm a bit afraid of what I might see."

Daphne took the phone. "I just scroll down?"

"Uh huh. Bit like a text message but more people involved."

There were more dings.

Daphne read aloud.

"Desmond is the author. Sender. He says you lot are in for a shock."

"That's what he said?" John asked.

"There's already replies so I'll read them in order." Daphne sat on the grass beside Ilona. The messages were going back and forth at speed.

Tracy: Feeling bored, Des? Read a book.

Desmond: Nobody asked you.

Tracy: You did. You said, 'you lot' and I am part of this chat.

Sonia: Is there any point to this?

Tracy: Nope.

Desmond: Fine. But I know what just happened at Edwina's.

Daphne glanced up. "There's some angry faces from both Tracy and Sonia. Who else is part of the chat, Ilona?"

"Fred. He won't be thrilled if Desmond is about to spill the beans. Me, of course. Constance. But she'll be working and won't touch her phone in the shop, good girl she is."

"There's more."

Desmond: Freddie's been a bad boy.

Tracy: Get to the facts.

Sonia: Is this about Mum?

Desmond: We should get together. Tell you in person.

Tracy: Hang on. If that's the case, come to the show. I can't leave.

Sonia: Is it about Mum?

Desmond: Let's meet at the show. Six?

Tracy: Five. Got the jam-off event at six. Better be worth it. I'm busy you know. Not like you two.

"Oh my. There's a poked tongue face thingy from Desmond. I thought these people were adults." Daphne raised both eyebrows. Ding. Ding. Ding.

Desmond: Be near the front gate at five. I'll bring the news.

Sonia: I'd rather watch grass grow.

Desmond: Then you also miss out on the truth about your father.

Ilona gasped and scrambled to her feet. "He can't tell her! Not there. And not without me as a support."

The group chat was off. "Tell her what?" Daphne asked. Was this the secret Desmond and Ilona had touched on at the park the other evening? She handed the phone back and caught Ilona's eye. "What is the truth about Sonia's father?"

But Ilona looked away. "Not for me to tell. Sorry."

"Does Sonia want to know?"

"She won't say. Edwina let her believe it was Fred but Desmond thinks he knows who it really is. Guess being neighbours for decades one might see things. But rather than dredging up the past, I believe these things are best left alone." Ilona walked towards the house, calling over her shoulder. "Need to check the sheep."

John held out his hands for Daphne. "What do you think."

She took them and climbed to her feet with only a couple of groans.

"About Desmond telling Sonia whatever this secret is? She deserves the truth. I know what it feels like to believe one thing and then discover it was all a lie. Not pleasant. But even if she wants to know, what if the real father doesn't want her to know? Or doesn't know himself? Now that could throw the cat among the pigeons."

Arm in arm, Daphne and John made their way back to their car. Ilona was nowhere to be seen. Porter was at the front door and nodded goodbye. John was quiet.

As they nosed down the road, Adam's patrol car went the other way and he waved.

John raised his hand in return. "Daph. Do you think it possible a man wouldn't want to know he had a daughter?"

Was he worrying so much about Sonia? How sweet of him.

"I have to wonder about a man who was involved with a woman and didn't stay around long enough to know he was a father. He might not be the kind of father a girl would want."

There was no answer from John. The wrinkling of his forehead was a giveaway that something was playing on his mind. Daphne patted his leg and he smiled. For a minute.

FRED'S EXPLANATION

As they waited to turn onto the main road to go back to Bluebell, a car rounded a curve on the wrong side of the road.

"Did you see that?" John shouted.

The car moved back into its lane and sped past.

Daphne had and she peered at the driver. "Is that Fred?"

"Think it is. Sorry I yelled. Shocked me."

"Follow him." Daphne said. "I think we should."

John glanced at her. He'd say no. He'd say they needed to mind their own business and not get any more involved in the goings on in Shady Bend than necessary. And he'd be right, of course.

But he grinned.

"You, my sweetheart, are a bad influence." He pulled onto the road and followed at a distance.

Well. Wonders do happen.

"He wasn't being very careful," she said. "Thank goodness nobody was coming the other way.

"Downright dangerous. Wonder if he's upset at having to come clean about Edwina."

With no indicator on, the car ahead turned into a side street.

"That's the way to the cottage." Daphne leaned forward. "Surely he wouldn't go back there?"

But he did. His car was halfway up the driveway when they drove past. John went a bit further along to where the road inclined and he did a U-turn.

"I can see the front of Edwina's cottage from here, love." Daphne pointed.

"Let's pull over. Might get my phone out."

John Jones you are becoming an excellent sleuth.

Car parked, they both got out and slipped beneath the cover of a tree. From this elevated spot, there was a view back to Shady Bend over trees and houses. It was interesting how the landscape varied between bushland and orchards.

"Wonder if he's visiting Sonia. Perhaps to tell her the truth." John trained his phone camera on Fred, who was out of his car but motionless at the bonnet. "He's staring at something."

"Any idea what?" Daphne couldn't tell from this distance but it was in the general direction of the garden. There was no other movement. Not even a rustle of branches because the air was still. She glanced up through the canopy. Although the sky was blue, she shivered. There might not be a storm coming but something else in this community was terribly wrong.

Fred moved towards the cottage then stopped again. He pulled something from a pocket.

"He's checking a message. I think." John relayed what he saw through the advantage of his zoomed in camera.

"Hopefully not checking the group chat!"

If Fred read what Desmond had said about him, who knew how he'd react. For that matter, what else was Fred hiding? In Daphne's experience, people rarely kept one secret. If they had something to hide it was likely to creep into many areas of their life and affect more than the main problem. And if he hid *how* Edwina died, was it possible he hid where she was now?

"John?"

"Can't see if he's on group chat. But he is scrolling so my guess is he is." John said.

"No. I mean, that's no good. But do you think we need to let Adam know that Fred is here? What if he tampers with anything?"

John lowered the phone to look at Daphne. "What's worrying you?"

"A feeling."

"About?"

"Fred is dishonest. He lied about something as important as a woman's death."

"And you are thinking about what else he's lied about?"

You know me so well.

She nodded.

"Why don't you send Adam a text message while I keep an eye on Fred?" John suggested.

"I will."

Daphne searched for Adam's number.

"Um…we might need to get back in the car." John pointed. "Sonia is heading his way and she's not looking happy to see him."

From around the corner of the cottage, Sonia stormed across the grass.

"Oh dear. Let's go."

By the time John parked beside Fred's car, the other two had vanished. But once they climbed out, it was easy to find them. Sonia was yelling at Fred.

"We should wait for Adam." John looked worried.

Daphne had finished her text message on the short car

ride but not heard anything back. Poor Adam must be tired of running from one place to the other thanks to this whole mess with Edwina.

"Don't you dare touch me!" Sonia screeched.

John was already running before Daphne took a step. So much for waiting. She puffed her way across the grass, skirting around the edge of garden beds and the bird bath.

Sonia and Fred were near the wall. Fred held his hands up near his shoulders, palms facing Sonia as if to prove he wasn't going to touch her. Sonia's face was distraught and tears poured down her face as she stepped side to side in agitation, arms wrapped around her body. She glanced at John and Daphne as they halted nearby then back to Fred.

"You killed my mother."

"Of course not! What a ridiculous thing to say, Sonia. You know I considered Edwina a dear friend after the divorce. But I did make a mistake, a big error of judgement, and for that I am so sorry."

Daphne put a hand on John's arm and they exchanged a quick look. Hopefully he understood she wanted to listen and only intervene if absolutely necessary.

"Mistake? Mum didn't have a heart attack and now we might never know what really happened. Why would you lie about something so important? You were married to her. And I always thought you cared about her."

"It's because I cared about her that I covered up what happened. Sonia, I wanted to protect her reputation."

Sonia stopped stepping side to side and dropped her arms. She waited for Fred to continue but he didn't, instead, he turned his attention to Daphne.

"Why are you both here?"

"We—"

"You meddled in my business. Followed me and hid in the bushes, no less, taking photographs of a private moment. And now everything has to come out about Edwina."

John took a step in front of Daphne. "Let's all stay calm."

Calm? Daphne's heart raced too fast to be calm. Being confronted was uncomfortable and upsetting but she'd done nothing wrong and if anyone should be hanging their head it was Fred.

An uneasy silence fell. Fred glared at John.

"Fred, tell me what really happened to Mum. Tell me now." Sonia's tears had stopped and she blew her nose. "What about her reputation?"

From his defensive stance and angry expression, it was unlikely he was going to say anything.

Then Sonia reached out and took Fred's hand. "Please. For my sake, please tell me what really happened."

Yes, Fred. Tell us all.

As quickly as he'd angered, Fred returned to his normal demeanour. Quiet. Respectful in his manner. The corners of his mouth curled up as he shot an apologetic look at Daphne. Whatever his faults, he cared for Sonia.

"I should have told you from the start."

"Told me what? You make it sound as though Mum was doing something illegal."

"No. Nothing like that." Fred sighed and took a few steps away from the wall. "I did find her there." He gestured. "But she'd fallen. Hit her head. There was quite a cut and I reckon she felt nothing. It was quick."

Sonia's forehead was deeply creased. "I don't understand. Why not just say so?"

"Because she'd been drinking. A lot by the look of the empty bottle where I found her."

"Mum didn't drink. You know she always said the driver who caused the accident had to be drunk to hit the car we were in and keep going. She swore off alcohol."

"Well, she was drinking. Between that and her heart meds it must have messed with her balance because she'd hit the wall and passed away within minutes. At least, that's what the doctor said. I didn't want people thinking badly of her. I didn't want you thinking badly of her, Sonia. Not as the last memory of your mum."

A doctor went along with this?

Not the time to ask. Sonia was weeping again and Fred put his arms around her. It was a touching moment but Daphne had a whole notebook of new questions to attend to. She leaned near John and whispered, "Shall we go?"

"Can you understand why I lied, Sonia? Please say yes." Fred's voice was gentle.

"Kinda. But it hurts you didn't tell the truth."

"No more lies, Sonia. I promise."

"We missed lunch, doll. Let me make us something now." It would keep him busy for a few minutes. Give Daph a chance to pull her thoughts together and write down some thoughts.

She was at the table, notebook open and pen turning in her fingers. "Just some tea would be lovely. But you have something."

He wasn't hungry.

Too much was playing on his mind. Not to mention his churning stomach. After filling the kettle and leaving it to boil, he went through the motions of adding tea leaves to the teapot and getting out the cups and saucers. In case Daphne was hungrier than she realised, he opened the container she kept her cookies in and placed it in the middle of the table. It didn't matter that they weren't the best cookies in the world. She made them with love and to him, that alone outweighed any shortcomings they had.

"What are your thoughts, love?" Daphne helped herself to a cookie. "What a strange series of events."

"Strange indeed. And I think it raises more questions."

"Agree. Do you think Fred will be in trouble with the police for lying? Would it be considered obstruction of an investigation?"

"Better answered by someone with legal training but I can't imagine he wouldn't be censured on one level or another. And think of the damage to his own reputation let alone if he finds himself in breach of professional codes of conduct."

Once the tea was ready, John joined Daphne at the table. She'd filled a page.

"Care to share?" he asked.

"There are so many moving parts, John. People withholding the truth. Others stirring things up to amuse themselves. And good people like Ilona seemingly caught in the middle. I'm trying to work out if Edwina's disappearance has anything in common with the three unfortunate deaths."

Daphne used the end of the pen to point at the top line. "Fred is connected to each person who has died in Shady Bend in the last few days. Putting aside the fact of him living in a very small town and knowing everyone, I feel this deserves a closer look. He found Edwina. Petra was a pallbearer and helped set things up for the wake. Zeke worked for Fred. And Amanda…" she trailed off with a thoughtful expression. "What does she have in common with all of this?"

"You told me when she arrived at the pre-funeral gathering that she was not expected and some people were surprised at her appearing." John said. "But at the actual wake, she was helping with the food. Didn't you mention Fred made some odd comment about her?"

Daphne flicked back through several pages of notes. "Yes. He said Amanda has an over-active imagination. Yet he made scones for her and Zeke after he'd had words with the latter. Oh." Her mouth dropped open and her eyes met John's. "What if he poisoned them?"

"Poisoned Amanda and Zeke? Why would he do such a thing?"

"And Petra." Daphne added.

"Wait on. You're suggesting Fred not only made a false report about Edwina's death, and somehow lost her body, but he killed off three members of the community. Fred? The mild-mannered funeral director?"

"Hm." After putting down her pen, Daphne reached for her tea. "It is far-fetched. And really, there's no reason to believe those three died from anything other than a terrible accident. I wonder if Adam has any news about how they ingested the poison."

"No doubt he'd say if he did. Well, when he could because he's had a busy day."

"Yes. I might give him an hour or so and then call."

Call Adam? Not a good idea.

Best to distract Daphne. "Tell me what else you've been writing down. Here, have another cookie."

CHASING THE TRUTH

The second cookie wasn't nearly as tasty as Daphne expected and she left most of it on the plate. Recently she'd begun to critically observe the flavours she came up with and this one just didn't seem to work. John, on the other hand, was munching his as if it were the most delicious thing he'd ever tasted.

"I may have gone overboard with the vanilla."

John shook his head and did a thumbs up.

Whatever is going on, John?

If it was the mystery then she'd back off. Upsetting her husband was at the bottom of the list of things she didn't like to do. Not just at the bottom, but buried far beneath layers of concrete. Concrete reinforced with titanium or whatever the strongest steel might be. With a deep and murky swamp on top for good measure. With crocodiles.

She giggled and John looked at her over the top of his glasses.

"What is the strongest steel?" she asked.

He blinked. "Titanium? I can find out."

"I'm being silly. My mind is at the point of going around

in circles which occasionally leads to strange places. Going back to this," she tapped the notebook. "What interests me is why a doctor signed a certificate supporting Fred's original claim about Edwina. Surely, they'd be required to do a proper examination and something such as a head wound must raise questions. Well, I think it would."

"Unless there was no doctor."

John had one of those expressions on his face. The lines on his forehead creased more than usual as he contemplated the problem. Daphne could guarantee his own mind was working overtime. He poured them both more tea and continued.

"Hear me out. Fred arrives at Edwina's after dark, which is quite late at this time of year. She's sadly passed away. At first, he thinks she's succumbed to a known heart condition but perhaps he touches her—they'd been married and he might have reacted without thinking. At this point he notices the head injury or possibly smells alcohol. Instead of actually calling for a doctor, he takes her to the funeral home and tidies her up."

"Then calls a doctor?"

"Yes. Someone he trusts."

She had another thought. "Or he called this trusted doctor, told them he'd found Edwina, possibly even sent a photo of her, and they signed the certificate without even coming to her place."

Who would do such a thing?

"We should ask Adam who the doctor was."

John took her hand. "No. No, he has enough to contend with. Between missing bodies, mystery deaths, and dishonest funeral home directors, he doesn't need us adding to his burden."

The phone rang.

"Speaking of Adam…" Daphne answered. "Just the man I

want to speak with. I'm popping you onto speaker if you don't mind. John's here." She placed the phone between them.

"Daphne. Hello, John. Why do you need to speak to me?"

John leaned forward. "Nothing urgent. What can we do to help?"

Nothing urgent? What is more urgent than solving this case?

Adam's voice sounded tired, even through the phone. "Sorry to bother you both."

"Never a bother." Daphne said. "Was everything alright when you arrived? We thought it best to let you know what was going on."

"You did the right thing. I had clearly told Fred to stay away from the property and make himself available for another interview once Detective Malone arrives back from another enquiry. He was waiting in his car when I got here and is upset he lost his temper with you."

"Will he be in trouble over this?" Daphne asked.

"Can't say. I thought you'd like to know we received a report about the source of the poison."

Both of them leaned forward to better listen.

"Seems to be from jam."

Daphne gasped.

"I know. You thought that from the beginning." Adam said. "Looks as though somebody added apricot kernels to their batch. Not a good idea at the best of times. There is a poison called…um, amygdalin inside the kernel. Nasty stuff."

"Adam, do you know where it came from? And if there's any still around?"

He sighed heavily. "Sad to say we located several suspicious jars in Petra's kitchen."

Or somebody might have planted them there.

"Ilona recognised the house key John found." Daphne said. "Someone had been in her house so what if that someone was leaving something behind instead of stealing anything? And the same someone trashed the place to make it look like a robbery."

Adam chuckled.

Daphne frowned.

"You've missed your calling, Daphne. I'm considering all possibilities. Petra's not here to defend herself so we have to take great care to look at things from all sides."

"I don't mean to step on your toes." She hadn't intended to take offence but was sure Adam and John both heard it in her voice. "You are a wonderful police officer and very good at your job."

"You're not stepping on anything. And you are too kind. There are some who think the opposite of me so I'll happily take the compliment."

Did he mean Tracy? Daphne knew in her bones there was nothing corrupt about Adam Browne.

John cleared his throat. "Quick question, Adam. Any chance this was all a terrible accident? Petra might have miscalculated the ingredients and then brought a jar along to the wake with no clue she was about to poison herself?"

"Not just herself." Daphne added. "When Amanda and Zeke had scones in the kitchen with Fred, they must have used the same jar. Fred was lucky."

There were voices in the background from Adam's end of the call. "I'm going to have to go. Detective Malone is here and Fred just arrived. But yes, it is possible it wasn't deliberate. I'll be in touch." He hung up.

As Daphne retrieved her phone, John stood. "Might make us another pot. Got a feeling we're going to need it."

"There's a fair bit of info about apricot kernels online, Daph." John's laptop was open and he scrolled with one hand while holding an almost empty teacup with the other. "Some people believe they can assist with cancer treatments."

"Even though they're toxic?"

"All about the dosage. And there are techniques for making jam which include the use of them. Not recommended but I wonder if that's what happened and too much was used?"

There were so many 'what ifs' right now. Enough to have covered a whole page of her notebook.

"Something is missing, John. There must be a connection between all of these seemingly separate issues. For example, we have a tussle over the secret recipe for a sauce with nobody admitting to having it."

"Although Sonia implied she does."

"Correct. Then there are two people who are allegedly at odds over their jam making skills to the point of a competition being organised to decide the victor but it must have been a front. A cover for the fact Petra made Edwina's products. I do wonder why not make them under her own label if they were so good?"

John swilled around the last of his tea. "Edwina had the name. The reputation. And the shop. Petra, on the other hand, owed people money and kept her little blackmail book. Maybe Edwina made Petra pay her debt off by working for her."

"So where is the book?" Daphne felt her mouth drop open. Was it really with the police or was that a lie? Who had told her...Tracy?

"Hellooo...anyone home?" Ilona called from outside.

"Come in, dear."

Ilona closed the door after herself. "Think we'll get a storm? So humid."

"Take a seat." John closed his laptop and stood. "Would you like some tea? Or we have some nice apple cider."

"Ooh, apple cider sounds good, thank you." Ilona slid opposite Daphne and glanced at the notebook. "Preparing for the next ceremony?"

"This is my list of questions about what's going on in this little town." Daphne closed the book. "Speculation. Did you sort out the fence at Petra's?"

"Yes, with a hand from one of the police. Both of us ended up covered in mud but the sheep are safe again. Can't go into Petra's until the forensic people finish and I'll be glad to tidy up for her. Well, not for her. But you know what I mean."

John placed a glass on the table then joined Daphne on her side.

"Thanks. I need to apologise for running off earlier. At Petra's. Sometimes my feelings get too much and I'm better off being alone for a bit. Like after the casket dropped at the funeral and they realised Edie wasn't inside. Anyway, I can't tell you who Sonia's father is because I don't know. Edwina never said it and I never asked."

Daphne nodded. "I can understand you being protective of Sonia. Does everyone think she has custody of Edwina's secret recipe?"

Ilona erupted into peals of laughter.

Had this all been a bit too much for her?

Picking up her glass, Ilona got the giggles under control and took a sip. "Sonia has nothing to do with the recipe. She doesn't even like the taste of it but what she does like is stirring up Tracy and some of the others. Even Fred believes Sonia has it. But can you imagine anyone keeping something so important on a handwritten note and only having one copy?"

"Do you know who has it?" Daphne asked. It was worth

the question. Ilona was close to the recipe's creator and had good local knowledge. "Did Petra make the sauce as well?"

"Petra was talented but I doubt she had the finesse for it. Can't really say." She looked at her drink.

"So you know, but prefer to keep the information private?"

Looking up again, Ilona frowned. "It isn't my secret to reveal. And until we find where Edie is, it seems wrong to bring it out in the open. I imagine she covers the recipe in her will. Same as the property and the shop."

"I keep hearing there is no will." John said.

"Oh, there is. But I genuinely have no idea who has a copy. If her solicitor doesn't, and Sonia doesn't, then who would?" Ilona finished her drink.

"Fred?" Daphne suggested.

"No. They might have given the appearance of remaining friends but I can assure you it was for Sonia's benefit. She might have known Fred wasn't her biological dad, but he did okay as a stepfather and after the car accident, stability was paramount to keeping Sonia from going off the deep end. Edie used to say to me it was his best feature, the way he treated Sonia." She smiled. "Fred and Sonia were closer than Edie and Sonia. Edie kept everyone at a distance and she wasn't perfect, but I loved her."

A buzzing sound took Ilona's attention and she pulled a phone from her pocket. "My reminder. Have another house to visit to put some chickens away in case we do get a storm later." She got to her feet. "Thanks for the drink, and the chat. Will I see you before you leave?"

Daphne and John got up as well, and John opened the door and climbed down. The women followed.

"We're heading out early, aren't we, John?" Daphne asked.

"Mid-morning. At the latest."

That late?

"Well, it's probably too much to hope for, but I'd like to think Edwina will be found before you go. And whoever broke into Petra's house."

John shaded his eyes from the sun. "Did you work out how the house key got into the wrong hands? You were quite adamant it was her own copy."

Ilona shook her head. "Oddest thing. All I can think is it fell from her handbag at or after the funeral and someone took advantage of it. Bit strange there was only that key found. Got to run. I'll send you a message later, if you like, once this little meeting at the show happens? Update you."

"Yes, please. Is it at five?"

"I think." Her phone buzzed again. "See you later!"

She sprinted away.

"Does she have to run everywhere? She's making me tired watching her!" Daphne said. John didn't answer. He was gazing into the distance, arms crossed. Thinking.

A GRAVE AFFAIR

"Wonder if we should have brought flowers. Not that she's there yet, but with the grave filled in and the headstone already installed..."

Daphne and John were in Shady Bend Cemetery and had stopped near Edwina's designated resting place. There was a temporary fence around it and a sign to keep off. Not that anyone would want to step all over an unfinished plot. Surely.

"I'm sure there will be plenty of floral tributes once she's found." John said.

"You know, I have the strangest sensation about this. As if I know where she is but can't quite put the thought together enough to make sense."

John took Daphne's hand and they headed away from the plot. "I understand what you mean. Which is why we're here."

About time he explained. After Ilona left, he'd barely said a word, just gone back into Bluebell and washed up the teacups and glass. Daphne left him to work through whatever was troubling him and drew a picture in her notebook. It was a very rough map of from where the police station stood at one end of the town to where they'd seen Ilona and Desmond in the park the other night. Halfway through adding comments, John picked up the car keys.

And now, with no explanation other than he needed to visit the cemetery, here they were. They went up to the trees at the top of the low hill.

"Care to fill me in?" she asked, a little out of breath. Low hill it might be but John had gone at a cracking pace.

"Something happened after the casket was dropped. Something I saw from up here, where I was doing my research." He gazed around. "Over here a bit."

There was a clear view of the area further down. Edwina's grave. The carpark.

"So, what did you see, love? I remember you running down the hill when everyone was screaming and carrying on. Was it then?"

With a shake of his head, John wandered to a tree. He stood there, staring at the base of the trunk.

"I was talking to Ilona. Remember how she ran up here, all distressed? I found her when I came to retrieve my notebook which I'd dropped in the earlier panic." Once again, John gazed in the distance. Towards the carpark.

He'd come up here when Petra was being loaded onto the stretcher. Everyone was fussing around her. Tracy was looking for something.

"Where is her handbag." Daphne said.

"What did you say?" John's full attention was on Daphne and she searched her memories.

"Tracy said Petra would need her phone and wallet and stuff at the hospital. As a pallbearer she'd left everything in the hearse."

"In her handbag?"

"Yes. Fred went to get it…oh, John!"

Their eyes locked together.

"Daph, I remember. Petra's handbag was on the stretcher with her."

"After Fred went to get it from the hearse. And he took a while."

"Long enough to get a key off a keyring?"

There was no need to respond. They both knew the answer.

They'd sat in the car for a few minutes, each deep in their own thoughts. Daphne suspected who'd broken into Petra's house. But why? Why would Fred do such a thing? Taking a key from an ill woman's handbag implied he already had a plan in mind.

"John? Assuming Fred took her house key just after Petra collapsed, one has to ask whether he was responsible for her death."

"Maybe. But how could he be certain she'd pass away? Even if he'd poisoned her, she was alive when the paramedics were leaving so why would getting her house key matter so much?"

"We need to ask Adam if all of Petra's keys are missing." Daphne reached for her phone.

"I think we should work this out before talking to the police. Last thing we want is to offer a half-baked idea." John didn't look at Daphne and again, she sensed something wasn't right.

Casting her mind back, she recalled this part-distracted, part-withdrawal of John's began when he'd returned to the police station to collect his phone. He'd stood outside with Adam for a moment in discussion. Had something been said which he didn't want to discuss with her? Something about the case.

"Love?" Daphne took one of his hands. "Please tell me what's troubling you. I wouldn't press, but lately you've been quiet and even worried. Is it because I'm getting involved where I shouldn't? Because I'll stop and we can leave right now, and—"

"I'm okay." John smiled and squeezed her hand. "I am thinking something through but it isn't about the case and I think we need to stay tonight."

"But you're not going to share what the problem is."

"I promise I will. Very soon." He leaned over and kissed her lips. "Trust me."

"I do trust you."

But I want to know!

"Going back to the problem at hand, we both agree we saw Fred with Petra's handbag on the day of the funeral. The day Petra collapsed."

Daphne wound down her window. If they were going to sit in the car, she needed some fresh air.

"If the police find he did remove her house key and use it, what was the purpose?"

"Plant the jars of poisonous jam. Look for the blackmail book." Daphne said. "Petra might have kept notes about Fred. Maybe suspected he was up to no good. I really feel we need to bring this to Adam's attention. Didn't he say they were interviewing Fred at the moment?"

Sonia walked past, not seeing them as she carried a huge bouquet of yellow roses towards Edwina's grave. She climbed through the temporary fencing and stood for a moment or two, eyes on the headstone. Then, she placed the flowers on the ground and climbed back out without a back-

The Shadow of Daph

ward glance. Halfway back to the carpark, she answered a phone call and walked as she talked.

"Left Mum some flowers…is there still no news?"

"We shouldn't listen." John whispered.

Daphne pretended she hadn't heard.

"I never said you were responsible for her going missing, Fred. Never." Sonia stopped and turned to face the cemetery.

Very thoughtful of you to stand within earshot.

"You told them what?"

Daphne would have given anything to hear the other end of the conversation.

"But why would Zeke and Amanda steal Mum? You can't really believe that! And then what? They simultaneously took poison out of remorse…yes, I am being sarcastic."

She listened for a while and her shoulders slumped. Her head nodded a couple of times. "Okay, okay. Whatever, Fred. I'm not up for this." She hung up and then squatted, dropping her head into her hands.

Before she could stop herself, or John could, Daphne was out of the car. Poor Sonia. So much to deal with and now the one person she trusted was proving less than honest.

"Sonia? It's just Daphne."

Sonia glanced over her shoulder.

"John and I were in our car. Just over there. We didn't mean to overhear but you seem sad." Daphne reached Sonia and went in front of her. She knew better than to attempt to squat. There'd be no coming back from such a risky manoeuvre.

"I bet you got a kick out of eavesdropping."

"It wasn't intentional, dear. You walked right past us with those lovely roses earlier."

With an exaggerated sigh, Sonia straightened and glanced at the car. John was near the bonnet, tapping on his phone.

"Fine. You didn't mean to listen in on my private conversation. I suppose you have questions. I mean, aren't you some kind of super sleuth or something? That's what Ilona's cousin said to her."

"Hardly. Just a keen observer of humans. All I came over for was to ask if you are doing okay. There's been such a lot for you to deal with between losing your mother—"

"Literally. Go on."

"Yes, well. And the three friends in quick succession. And Fred's revelation about how he really found your mother."

"I wish somebody would find Mum now. Let her rest properly. But the others weren't my friends. Petra did stuff for Mum. Same as Desmond. And others. But Petra was sneaky and not very nice. Zeke was okay but he'd do whatever Amanda told him to and as for her…" Sonia's eyes hardened. "Good riddance."

Oh my!

Daphne stepped back at the venom in the other woman's tone.

"She was useless helping Mum with her heart condition. Signed prescriptions for her without even checking her pulse or running any tests. I wish she had lost her licence instead of just leaving the practice."

As quickly as she'd angered, her mood shifted and again, her shoulders slumped. After a look back at the grave, Sonia walked past Daphne who was trying to process what she'd just heard.

"Sonia, wait a minute." Daphne followed. "One question and I won't trouble you any further." She caught up with Sonia at an old mini. "Do you know who signed your mother's Cause of Death certificate?"

Driver's door open, Sonia stopped long enough to roll her eyes. "Not very smart for a sleuth, are you? Who else but her own doctor. Amanda signed it of course."

As Sonia drove out of the car park, Daphne's mind was in overdrive. And the direction it was taking was disturbing. Very disturbing indeed.

HANDBAGS AND ROSES

"Adam's flat out, Mrs Jones." Porter attended the counter at the police station. She was alone from the look of things. "He's with the forensic investigators and could be hours yet, so unless it is urgent?"

"John and I recalled something from the funeral and thought it might be useful information." Was this a mistake? She and John might put two and two together and come up with four, but since when did the police—trained investigators doing their job—need the advice of a retired couple with too much time on their hands? "I'm sorry. I don't mean to waste your time and should let you get back to work."

Daphne forced a smile and made for the front door. This was twice today she'd doubted her reasoning. Seen herself from another perspective. A meddler. A nuisance who was tolerated because she'd been unwittingly put in the middle of events.

"Mrs Jones? Daphne, I'm happy to leave a note for Adam. We can use all the help we can get."

"You're sure? I don't wish to be a pest."

Porter laughed. "That is the last thing you are. You've helped a lot so come and tell me what's on your mind."

John was outside. He'd mentioned needing to make a phone call and after all the texting at the cemetery, Daphne had the feeling it might be to do with their real estate agency back in Rivers End. Although the young man running things was capable, on occasion he and John conferred about properties or clients.

"Very well." Daphne placed her handbag on the counter. "I'm not expecting you to tell me any details, but if you haven't already uncovered how Petra's house key got into the hands of the person who entered and trashed her house, then we may have the answer."

Porter raised her eyebrows. "Let me grab a notepad." She went to her desk. "On my own at the moment. Too much going on in our little town and we've had to split the resources."

"Between Petra's house and Edwina's house?"

"Oh, not Edwina's. They're finished up there. But yes, Petra's house as well as back at the funeral home." She returned, opened the notepad and pulled a pen out of a plastic cup on the counter. "Right. Go ahead."

"On the day of the funeral, I was officiating, as you know. John—my husband—was in the cemetery as well. Genealogy is his hobby and he was up the little hill. If we fast forward to after the casket was dropped and after Petra collapsed, both of us observed the same person with her handbag. We just hadn't compared notes and in fact, John hadn't given it any thought until we were back up there today and it jogged his memory."

"I'm all ears."

"The paramedics were putting Petra onto the stretcher and Tracy was looking for her belongings. Said she'd need her phone and purse at the hospital."

"So, it was Tracy with the handbag?"

"Negatory. It was Fred."

Pen poised to write, Porter's eyes shot back to Daphne's.

"Say again."

"I heard Fred say he'd collect Petra's handbag from the hearse. And John saw him give it to the paramedics who placed it beside her. Now we certainly don't know that he removed the key but he did take a few minutes to retrieve the handbag."

After jotting down a few lines, Porter pulled out her phone. "Just a minute, please." She wrote and sent a message. "I've let Adam know. He's at the funeral home with the dogs again. Well, one dog."

"Oh, let me guess. The one who took such a dislike to Fred the other day."

"Got it in one."

"Fred told us he didn't like dogs and the police dog must have sensed it. But it struck me as odd that the dog couldn't pick up the trail of someone who'd been at the funeral home for several days—Edwina—yet was so intent on Fred. Did you ever find the rhubarb and apricot jam Petra ate the day of the funeral?"

"No. We did look even though the staff did a search as soon as Adam alerted them to the possibility the jar was contaminated. Fred was adamant there was none of that flavour on the premises."

"Fred?"

Was that why the police dog was so upset? What if Fred had handled the jar to dispose of it and the dog could sense the poison?

"Mrs Jones. Daphne. I'm going to have to make some phone calls if you could excuse me. Unless you have more information?"

Porter's expression begged Daphne to leave. She fiddled

with the pen and glanced at her phone. She might be thinking the same thoughts and not give anything away to a civilian.

"No, dear. Well, apart from Sonia telling me that Amanda signed Edwina's Cause of Death certificate. Which seems a bit convenient."

"Sorry. How?"

"Did Amanda even attend the cottage that night? She signed something to say Edwina died from a heart condition. But Fred admitted Edwina had a head injury which wasn't included on the certificate. Do we even know for certain Amanda saw the body?"

Porter's phone beeped but she ignored it. "Are you thinking Fred had something to do with Edwina's death?"

"Surely it is possible. And if Amanda lied, then Fred might have needed to make sure the truth never came out."

"You think he poisoned Amanda. What about Petra and Zeke?" Beth's phone rang.

"I'll leave you with that thought."

No point keeping Constable Porter from answering her call. Daphne had said her piece. If there was anything useful in it, then she had to trust the police would add it to their information base. It was out of her hands. She'd done enough and it was time to head back to Bluebell for their last night here.

When Daphne emerged from the police station, she wore a look of satisfaction which brought John a moment of relief. He'd wanted to be in there with her for support and to back up her statement. But there was someone he needed to speak with and the timing clashed. Whether he'd made the right decision remained to be seen.

"Finished with your call?" Daphne joined him beneath a tree near the car. "Everything alright?"

"Yes, and yes. Would you care for a cold drink at the café?"

"Yes please!"

Leaving the car where it was, they crossed the road but the café was closed and John checked his watch. "Goodness me. Hadn't noticed how late it is. They closed an hour ago so what about some bottled water from the supermarket?"

They decided to walk the block or so as the weather was finally cooling down and as they did, Daphne repeated the conversation with Porter.

"She seemed shocked about Fred handling Petra's handbag. Oh, and the police dog, the one which disliked Fred, is back at the funeral home for some reason. Wouldn't be surprised if there's an arrest in the cards."

Once they had their water, they sat on a bench beneath the awning of another shop. The street was quiet as the day wound down. Shady Bend was a nice place to visit. To sit for a while. Or would be if there wasn't at least one criminal on the loose.

"It was different in Little Bridges," Daphne said. "There was a family feud and it made it so much easier to pinpoint who had real motive to kill, even though it was a surprise once we found out. But here, well there isn't a clear picture of why this happened."

"Edwina? Or the others?"

"Still feel it is all connected. When I was at the cottage for Sonia's photo shoot, I wondered how someone who cared so much for their garden would let other aspects of their life fall apart. I think that garden is at risk of falling apart." Daphne sighed and opened her water bottle.

"I don't understand? Do you think it won't be cared for?"

"Not going by the poor roses." Daphne said.

"Which roses?"

"Oh, the ones from the postcard. Remember I said Sonia insisted we have our photo taken in front of them and I noticed the middle three or four plants were on the droopy side. I took a photo."

She took her phone out and scrolled through her gallery. "Here we go. See how the leaves look so sad. And it was only these four in the middle. Not so obvious from a distance." Daphne found an image of the whole rose bed.

"That's not right."

"I know. Almost as if someone watered the ones on each end and not the middle."

John shook his head. "I mean the colours. I'm sure in the large photograph at the show that the roses were alternating. Pink, yellow, red. See how each one on the end is red, then the next is yellow, then pink and so on until we get to these four."

Red, yellow, pink, red became red, red, pink, yellow.

He used his fingers to pinch the screen and zoom in, this time to the ground beneath the roses.

"New mulch on those roses. Look, the mulch under the others is faded but under those central four or five there's a fresh covering. Could be they're not getting enough water beneath it. But the colours..."

He was certain he was right. He'd loved the photo at the show and paid it quite a lot of attention, enjoying the little touches in it, such as the patterns of colours.

"I know how we can check." Daphne said as she stood.

"Not sure we should be going to the cottage."

"Didn't you buy a postcard of the same photograph?"

"Clever cookie. Yes, I did." John got to his feet. "We can drive home and take a look."

"Or, seeing how close we are to Edwina's shop, we could drop in and take a look at the postcard stand."

John put an arm around Daphne's shoulders and kissed her cheek. "Even better."

He was probably wrong. There was no reason to believe there was anything out of place in the rose garden. Apart from droopy leaves, new mulch, and the possibility of roses dug up and replanted. Nothing out of place at all.

IN HER GARDEN

"I wonder why the canine unit is back at the funeral home. Do you think they're searching for Edwina again, or trying to find if there is any more poisonous jam hidden away?" Daphne asked as they crossed the last street before Edwina's shop.

"Good question. Guess it depends on what came of the interview with Fred as well as any forensic results the police have had in."

A car slowed as it passed them. Fred glared through the window at Daphne and a shiver shot up her spine. He'd probably had quite enough of seeing her wherever he went. Well, they'd be gone soon and she, for one, wasn't going to miss the funeral home director. As nice as he'd been to her in the beginning, it was becoming clear there was more to the man than met the eye. For all she knew, he might have murdered Edwina and the other three.

"Okay?" John opened the door to the shop. "You look a bit troubled."

No point worrying you with my silly thoughts.

"I really like some of the people here. And the area. I'd like to come back one day but only as a tourist."

"Did you say tourist?" Constance welcomed them with a huge smile. "I love tourists. I love every customer actually and am so happy you've both returned for more of our delectable goodies."

It was like seeing a dear friend again, stepping in here. The same sense of familiarity from the other day returned and Daphne's heart filled up at the genuine friendliness of the young woman.

"We'd love to see what else you have, not that we've had a chance yet to open even one of the products from the last visit."

"Not even the special sauce?" Constance asked in surprise.

"Special occasion. You did mention it was in short supply." John wandered over to the postcards. "Do you happen to know when the photo was taken from this one?" He picked up the postcard of Edwina's garden and cottage. "How long ago?"

"About a month ago. Sonia showed it to Edwina on her phone the day she took it, here in the shop. She was so happy but Edwina told her she should have waited until the cottage was repainted. They had a bit of a spat about it because every year Edwina says she'll have it painted in summer and then it never happens. Sonia said she was entering it in the show and Edwina told her not to expect to win."

"It didn't." John said. He showed Daphne. "See the roses."

He had an excellent memory. The roses alternated between pink, yellow, and red. No two plants of the same colours were beside each other and the plants appeared strong and healthy.

Constance joined them, her eyes darting to the postcard. "Is something wrong?"

"Dear, are you aware of anyone moving these roses

around? Perhaps some of them were diseased or something and needed replacing?" Daphne asked.

"Haven't heard anything like that and I'm sure Edwina would have told me. She talked about her garden more than anything else and there is no way her plants would be diseased or the like. If she wasn't in the garden, she was talking about it which is why some of us..." Constance bit her lip.

"Daph, I might just make a quick call about that thing we discussed on the way here."

John went outside and as he dialled, he wandered out of sight.

"Which is why some of you do what?" Was Constance in on the arrangement of making products under Edwina's name? "John and I were at Petra's house earlier. Ilona asked us to go there while she waited for the police to arrive. Outside the front door was a box, a bit battered from being dropped by the delivery driver by the looks of things. But we could easily see the contents."

Constance abruptly turned and walked to the other side of the counter. Her lips were pressed against each other and her face had paled. She fussed with her apron for a while and Daphne gave her time to think.

"It's not what you think." Constance blurted. "Edwina was very talented but when she was diagnosed with her heart condition it was if everything changed for her. She lost interest in making her jams and preserves and even in painting. Some of us helped out. You need to understand Edwina made this town a destination and she was so afraid of letting it down. Of this shop failing because of her illness." Tears brightened her eyes.

"I didn't mean to upset you. How kind of you and the—others—to help keep things going. But now she's gone, people won't expect her name on products."

"There's so much to sort out. People are saying the shop won't continue to trade."

"It won't."

Both women swung around. Fred stood inside the door.

"What makes you think that?" Daphne asked.

Her heart pounded but she wasn't about to allow this man to stop her finding the truth despite his somewhat belligerent stance with his legs apart and arms crossed.

Trust yourself, Daph. Be brave.

"Fred, why wouldn't the shop keep running?"

"The real question is why *would* it. Edwina is dead. Sonia doesn't want to run it. That leaves nobody. It'll be sold off to repay debt."

"What kind of debt?" Daph asked. John came into view outside, still on the phone. He glanced in and stopped when he saw Fred, who at that moment took a couple of steps forward. John said something and hung up the call.

"Me. She owed me money from our divorce and we had an arrangement that I'd be paid back out of the sale of this and that the property will come to me."

Constance laughed. This took Fred's attention away from Daphne and she quickly caught John's eye and did a tiny shake of her head. Fred might let something slip if he thought he had a limited audience.

"Nothing funny about this, Constance. You're about to lose your job and not even your bully of a father can stop that."

"Dad isn't a bully, Fred. And this shop isn't going anywhere."

"Is that right?" Fred sneered at Constance and Daphne stepped around the counter to stand beside her. "Look at the two of you. Think you're both so smart but I have letters signed by Edwina and without a will—"

"There is a will!"

"She never made one, Constance."

"It might be missing at the moment but I've seen it which is why I know this shop is safe and so is Sonia's home."

Fred's arms dropped to his sides and a strangely comical expression of confusion replaced his smugness. He shook his head. Muttered something. And then took another step.

John walked in. "I'm back, Daph. Have you got some more of the special sauce?"

Silence fell. John stayed near the door. Daphne grabbed Constance's hand behind the counter and squeezed it. Fred put both his hands on the counter, his eyes going from John to Constance.

In the distance, a siren wailed.

"This will. What does it say about the recipe?" Fred asked. "She owes it to me. I'm the one who supported her getting this place off the ground. I paid for everything when all she had was kitchen skills and a vision. Do you know I even poured money into her precious garden? And I raised someone else's child as my own."

Daphne released Constance's hand and forced herself to go around the end of the counter. John looked alarmed but she had questions to ask. Best done without a barrier.

"Sonia seems to care a great deal about you, Fred. Wouldn't you want her to keep the property she's always lived on?"

"The thing none of you understand is Desmond wants to buy the place to extend his orchard. He'll leave Sonia's cottage alone but bulldoze Edwina's and dig up her garden. But she told me I could have it if I keep her garden. Of course, I'll keep her garden." With something like a sob, Fred covered his face with his hands.

The siren was closer and John glanced through the window.

"Fred? When did Edwina say you could have the property?"

He dropped his hands and straightened. "Right before I pushed her. I didn't mean to. We were arguing about Desmond. Again. And she yelled at me I could have the blasted property but it would never change the fact he was Sonia's father."

Constance gasped and her hand flew to her mouth.

Not common knowledge then?

"I didn't mean to hurt her." Fred shook his head. "Never meant it."

The siren stopped.

"And you buried her in the rose garden." Daphne said with a calmness she certainly didn't feel. To the contrary, her legs shook and her stomach did somersaults. She'd need a lie down after this. "And Amanda signed a certificate without seeing her body."

He nodded. All the fight was gone. "Amanda was drunk and didn't even remember. At least not until Zeke mentioned not having to replace any embalming products like he normally would. He began to question whether Edwina was ever there so I paid him a bundle of cash to say he'd helped collect her and had seen her at the funeral home. But then he wanted more. Things went downhill fast."

Adam let himself in. His eyes shot to Constance who gave him a tiny smile. A little of the tension on his face drained away. Daphne wasn't finished but at least Adam was here to listen.

"So, Zeke wanted more hush money and he was involved with Amanda. You made them scones with jam and cream. Where was the jam from, Fred?" Daphne crossed her fingers behind her back. Would he keep talking now Adam was here?

As if he'd held onto secrets for too long, Fred poured it all out. "Petra did something with the apricot and rhubarb jam. She told me she found an old recipe using a small amount of ground apricot kernels and thought she'd add a few extra for good measure. Added it when the jam was almost cool. Silly woman didn't bother to check about the danger and by the time she told me, she'd already eaten some. I put the jar in my pocket intending to dispose of it but then she died."

"Were you afraid you'd be blamed?"

"I've said enough."

Adam stepped forward. "Fred, I need you to accompany me to the police station."

As if seeing Adam for the first time, Fred gazed up at him. "Three times in one day."

"You might have told me this earlier, mate." Adam took handcuffs out. "Do I need these?"

"Rather you didn't if you don't mind. Have a reputation to uphold."

Porter burst through the door, followed by another uniformed police officer. She stopped, looking from one to the other.

"Mind taking Fred in? Put him in the interrogation room and stand guard. I'll be along soon."

Fred stumbled out with the other two officers holding his arms.

Adam hurried around the counter to wrap Constance in a hug. Over her shoulder, he nodded to Daphne and mouthed 'thank you'.

Those shaky legs weren't getting any better and Daphne grabbed at the counter top as they threatened to give away. John was there in an instant and slid his hands under her arms and Adam dragged a stool around from the back.

And then Daphne burst into tears.

NOT FAIR

After a glass of water and a small piece of fudge which Constance insisted she eat, Daphne was steady as a rock again. Or close enough.

"I'm going to go to the station and charge Fred." There was worry in Adam's eyes when he looked at Daphne. "Are you going straight home?"

John took Daphne's hand. "Just stopping long enough to get something easy for dinner and we'll head back. You don't need us for anything tonight? I'd like to get Daph home and fed."

Daphne laughed and the other three looked at her. "You make it sound like I'm an over-tired toddler. I'm fine, all of you stop worrying."

Constance gave her a quick hug. "You are amazing. The way you persuaded Fred to tell you all of his secrets was like watching a movie. A really good detective movie. Dad, what if I join the police force?"

"No."

Everyone laughed.

"Connie, isn't it closing time? Do you want me to stay?" Adam glanced at his watch.

"Go arrest Fred. I'll close up and then I'm going to the show."

After Adam left, John grabbed the shop sign from outside for Constance.

"Are you sure you are doing alright, dear? That was quite a shock." Daphne asked.

"Oh, I'm fine. But I'd never have guessed Fred was a killer and had no idea about Desmond. Does Sonia even know?"

"I think so. Well, he was going to tell her at five, wasn't he? At the gates to the show. Actually, do you need a lift there, Constance? We're going right past." John offered. "I can pop into the supermarket now and be back in five. If you're okay waiting, Daph?"

"Actually, a lift would be good. Meeting a friend so getting home is fine." Constance followed John to the front door. "I'll lock us in."

As Constance counted the takings, Daphne found herself drawn to the small oil paintings on the shelf. Was there anything left which Edwina really created? Any paintings, or produce? How sad to lose interest in a lifelong passion thanks to health concerns. And how kind of others to try and keep her wishes alive.

"May I ask something? And don't feel obliged to answer because I've already heard you refuse to tell Fred, but…"

Constance grinned as she folded a money bag. "The recipe for the secret sauce?"

"Am I that obvious?"

"It's what everyone wants to know." Constance leaned on the counter. "Tracy and Fred and Desmond and Petra. And others. Always asking Edwina to sell it to them. To let them commercialise it. And she would have except it was never hers to sell."

The smile on the younger woman's face said it all. There was a quiet pride in her expression and Daphne clapped her hands in delight.

"You created the recipe!"

"I did. And I was all of sixteen at the time so Dad and Edwina came to a legal arrangement about her selling it under the shop brand. I make it and take a sizeable share of the proceeds and now Edwina is gone, I'll receive documentation to prove my ownership. Once the current batch is sold, I will begin selling under my own label."

"You are clever as well as kind and friendly and brave and beautiful."

Constance blushed and picked up the money bag. "Must run in the family. I'll be right back." She disappeared into the back room.

Run in the family? Adam might be most of those things but Daphne wouldn't describe him as beautiful. Or did she mean her mother? Either way, Constance was a wonderful young woman and she was very pleased to know her. It made the whole time in Shady Bend worthwhile.

John was able to park not far from the front gate of the showgrounds to let Constance out.

"I'll see you tomorrow?" Constance climbed out. "Can't wait to go and see who the winners are."

"Have fun, and yes, we'll pop in before we leave." Daphne said.

Constance waved and walked away, then stopped to look at her phone. "Hey! I just got asked to be a surprise judge!"

"That's exciting! What for?"

"The jam-off event. Me, Ilona, and Tracy. See you!"

With that she was sprinting off.

John started the motor and Daphne's hand flung out to grip his knee.

"No. We have to stop her."

"Why would we do that?"

Daphne undid her seatbelt. "This jam-off is the event Fred designed to judge whether Edwina or Petra's jam was the best. But there's no competition because—"

"Petra made them both!" John turned off the motor and was out of the car in an instant. "It is almost six."

Daphne got out in a bit of a panic, spilling the contents of her handbag all over the ground. "Oh dear. John, you run after her. I don't have Connie's number so I'll phone Adam and Ilona and be right behind you."

By the time she'd thrown everything back in her bag, John was out of sight. Daphne paid for a ticket and tried to dial as she walked. Never a good idea and after almost colliding with a post, she stopped to one side of the path. Her hands were shaking so much she had to put her password back in twice and then rang Ilona. The call rang out. No message bank. She tried Tracy and this time it was picked up. Thank goodness.

"Tracy is busy. If you must bother her, leave a message but make it snappy."

"Oh no. Um, This is Daphne. Do not let anyone taste the jam! This is an emergency." She hung up. Tracy would likely ignore her anyway.

Adam didn't answer but Porter did, and promised to call Constance and send a patrol car. Now she could follow John. He'd likely have taken the quickest route which was straight through the side show. Daphne turned the other way. If she hurried, she'd get there in time. Her phone rang.

Heavy breathing. "Daph…"

"John! What's wrong!"

He sounded awful.

"I'm okay. Turned my ankle in a pothole. Can only hobble. You need to get there."

"But…yes. Okay. Going."

Chin up, Daphne shoved the phone in her handbag as she turned back. There was no chance of reaching that pavilion by six o'clock if she took the long way.

The side show loomed. First were fairy floss sellers and popcorn machines. Not a problem at all. Then some rides. Bumper cars. Giant teacups.

I could use a cup of tea. With a good splash of sherry in it!

Along here it was busy. Kids and adults and lots of teens all out for fun. Some lined up for rides and others for a chance to win something. Clown head turned side to side, mouths open to catch a ball. Disappointed faces mingled with excited ones.

She gulped, pushing down a giant lump of ice in her chest.

The music. The same music from the merry-go-round from the other day. And from her distant memories.

You have to save Constance!

One step. Two. Another.

Shouting. An angry man yelling.

"Daphne! Daphne, you show yourself!"

Heart in her mouth, Daphne spun around.

Nobody was calling her.

But now she was frozen in place, her feet stuck to the ground and her throat tight. Horses went up and down. Lights and music. Chaos.

"Can you help me find my daddy?" A small hand held Daphne's. She looked down in shock. It was a little boy, maybe five or six years old, with big, scared eyes.

People brushed past.

"What's your name?" she croaked.

"John."

The Shadow of Daph

"Well, that is a fine name, John. Let's find your dad."

Up past the merry-go-round was a show official, sauntering in the other direction.

"We'll ask the man with the orange vest. Okay?"

The little boy nodded and they started off.

Past the merry-go-round.

John gripped her hand. Poor little mite.

Past the Ferris wheel.

Almost out of the side show. The official was just ahead.

"Excuse me, there's a little boy—"

"John! John, I'm here, son."

From behind came the call. The little boy released her hand and was running. She couldn't look. But she had to.

A young man opened his arms as John ran towards him, little legs pumping to get there.

"Don't…hurt…him." She whispered, her arms drawing up around herself. "Don't hurt…"

John's father lifted him and spun him around with a broad smile. "Gotcha! Stay closer, dude. Thanks, lady!" He joined the crowd and John waved at her as they disappeared.

She touched her face. It was wet with tears. But deep inside something had changed. The lump of ice had melted. Whatever happened back then, all those years ago, didn't matter anymore. The man she'd known as her father wasn't like the dad of the little boy. But he'd still been the man she called Dad.

And the pavilion was only twenty metres away.

John's ankle shot pain up his leg every time he put weight on it but he couldn't stop. Daphne hadn't gone past him so she must have been too far behind to make it in time. He was sure six o'clock had come and gone and if they were too late to stop the jam-off, what would happen? Would there be time to get anyone to hospital? To counteract the poison?

He shuffled up the ramp holding the railing and finally made it through the doors, blinking as his eyes adjusted.

At the far end of the building was a table with people seated and a selection of jams in front of them. Constance scooped up a spoonful.

"Staaap!"

The entire pavilion hushed. People turned. And most importantly, Constance dropped the spoon with a clang.

A breath whooshed out of him as Daphne wound her way through onlookers until she reached the table. She picked up the lids and one by one, twisted them back on the jars. "There'll be no jam tasting today!"

FAMILIES AND FRIENDS

Even though John was awake early, he didn't go far from Bluebell. Instead, he opened a camp chair and sat outside the door. Before long he'd wake Daphne, but for now, he had some thinking to do.

In a couple of hours, there was a small chance Daphne might finally meet her biological father. She didn't know about it. And she didn't because there was no guarantee Alfie would be there at the arranged meeting place. His one phone call with the man was awkward and left John with more questions than ever. There'd not been animosity, but nor was there surprise or excitement.

Had he done the wrong thing by contacting Alfie without telling his wife? Recently, she'd made comments about not wanting to know a man who didn't care if he had a child. And John had a strong feeling Alfie knew about Daphne.

There was no going back, but the next question was whether to explain his actions before he took Daphne to the gazebo in the park, a place all parties agreed on. All parties being him and Alfie, and Adam and Constance. Or did he take her there and try to explain at the time? It seemed unfair on Daphne.

"Why are you so sad?" Daphne climbed down the steps, wrapped in her dressing gown with her hair all curly after a shower last night.

John stood, taking care with his sore ankle, and gave her a kiss. "Not sad. Thinking."

"About yesterday?"

"No."

She tilted her head with a question and the love in her eyes gave him the answers he sought.

"What if I make you some coffee and we sit and talk for a while. There's something you need to know."

To call the past few days eventful was an understatement, but John's news shadowed it all. Daphne sipped her coffee as he spoke, using the action to keep her from jumping in and asking questions. There'd be time for that.

"I managed to get his phone number but it took a few tries to reach him. And I really don't want to get your hopes up about him actually coming to meet with us. He has a reputation as a cranky old man, not my words, and apart from his woodworking shop is a reclusive type."

John was nervous about this. He should have told her he was following leads after her father and now she understood why he'd been so distracted.

"Daph? I hope I've done the right thing."

She put down her cup and took his hand. "You've done the right thing. I always wondered if part of your interest in genealogy was looking for him but I never expected him to be alive, let alone found. You're a fine detective, John Jones."

He didn't seem quite convinced.

"Nobody else would have done this. My mother refused to help me look. And my siblings…well, they thought I was disrespecting my stepfather by wanting to know more." She leaned towards him and squeezed his hand. "I now know he is alive. And if I get to meet him, that is icing on the cake."

At last, a smile broke though and John lifted her hand and kissed her fingers.

"In that case, are you up for a bit of a walk in an hour?"

As it was, Daphne drove them both. John had insisted he would still drive towing Bluebell later which would become a problem if he made his ankle worse by lots of walking. The drive only took a couple of minutes and they wandered to the gazebo, which was empty.

"Bit early, Daph. Let's sit."

"Will we get a chance to say goodbye to Constance on the way out?" Daphne perched on the edge of a seat as nerves suddenly flooded her. "Thank goodness we got to her in time."

"You got to her. Daph, I've rarely been as proud of you as yesterday when you not only faced your fears but smashed them. When I heard you tell everyone to stop what they were doing I was so relieved."

"I think it was 'staaap'. But it worked, even if Tracy kept saying I should leave and stop drinking."

"But to her credit, once she knew there was a real threat with the jam she was like a drill sergeant. Find a box. Tighten the lids. Secure the jars in the box. And she did apologise. Sort of."

Tracy's grunted, "Cheers. You did okay," was about as good as Daphne would get.

Ilona had been the opposite, thanking Daphne and John

over and over. And then weeping when Adam arrived and gave the news that they knew where Edwina was buried. Sonia was absent as was Desmond.

"She kind of knew, in her heart, that he was her father." Ilona had said. "Sonia wasn't upset and he stopped all the bluff and bravado and they went to get a coffee. I think they'll be fine."

Now, as a car nosed into the carpark, Daphne put the memories aside. Was this Alfie Browne? What would she say? Or do? Which question first? Her head was a riot of thoughts clashing against each other.

But it was only Adam in his patrol car. He climbed out and waved. Was it some development in the case? Did he need to arrange an interview?

"How does Adam know we're here?"

"Not just Adam, Daph."

She stood and stared.

Constance got out of the back seat and opened the passenger door. She also waved with a huge grin and the truth hit Daphne.

"They are my relatives?"

"Adam is your cousin, doll."

Her throat constricted and she stopped breathing. Her heart was beating but so fast it hurt.

A frail man with lots of white hair and a limp held onto Constance's arm as they crossed the grass beside Adam. Daphne couldn't stay still and ran towards them but she could barely see where she was going and took off her glasses to wipe away the offending tears.

"Hiya, cousin." Adam joked and gave her a hug. "Best surprise I've ever had."

Constance reached for Daphne's hand and placed it on her arm, where Alfie's hand rested. "Daphne Jones, let me introduce my great uncle, and your father, Mister Alfred Browne."

Steady brown eyes gazed back at her in a face worn by time. The smallest flicker at the edge of his lips told her everything she'd needed to know. She didn't need questions. And she didn't need answers just now. She had her dad.

"Adam tells me you helped bring Fred Yates to justice. Never liked him." Alfie held Daphne's hand as they sat alone on a bench. The others were over at the pond talking.

"I just observed some things."

"Not going to lie to you, Daphne. I knew about you. Always did. But I wasn't welcome and never was good with staying in one place. Not until I settled here."

"Where you grew up. And you had siblings here."

"Adam was a kid without a dad, due to my brother passing away. He made up a little for my mistake."

Every ounce of joy seeped out of Daphne. This was worse than never meeting him. She couldn't unhear his admission.

"What's wrong, lass. Look like someone stole your dreams."

"I was a…a mistake?"

Alfie frowned. And then he put his hands on her shoulders. "You are no mistake. Me leaving you? That was the biggest mistake of my life."

"When will you and John come back to visit? Or move here? That would be good! Ilona doesn't want to be a celebrant anymore so you can take over." Constance had her arm through Daphne's as they all walked to the cars.

"I have quite a few bookings for a while, but John and I will look at the schedule tonight and see where we can make visits."

"Well, there have to be a lot. Something happened yesterday."

"Oh?"

"Petra's book? The one everybody was so afraid of? Well, she gave it to Dad a few weeks ago because she was trying to work on herself. Stop being a pain. He promised to lock it up until she wanted it back and so he did. And he remembered about it last night and guess what was inside?"

I am scared to ask.

"Edwina's will. I'd say Edwina figured it was safe with Petra because few people liked her and they had their arrangement with the products. Anyway, she left me the shop so I'm going to be very busy taking it to the next level."

"Starting with Connie's Special Sauce."

Neither of them spoke until Daphne parked beside Bluebell. There'd been more tears with goodbyes and some for happiness and now there was a whole lot of planning ahead.

"Thank you, love." Daphne turned the engine off. "You've given me a family."

"Couldn't be happier. I'm just sorry we can't stay longer."

"Can't let my bride and groom down."

They climbed out.

"I'll prepare Bluebell for travel. Should be ready in half an hour or so."

Daphne stood in the sunshine watching him as he began the tasks he'd turned into a fine art over the past few months. How she loved this man. He'd been her rock for all their marriage and she knew him as well as any person could know another person.

And I can never repay you for doing what nobody else would. You found my father.

He'd helped make her whole. But she'd helped herself as well. Carnivals might not be her go-to but she'd never fear them again.

"Everything okay? Maybe you should get out of the sun."

"Negatory. I think its high time I stepped out of the shade."

NEXT… TALES OF LIFE AND DAPH

A retreat in the mountains sounds perfect with spa treatments for Daphne and fishing for John. Until a killer strikes…

Daphne Jones is invited to an exclusive conference in the high country in Victoria. The annual meeting of wedding officiants is her first and she's excited to attend sessions with her peers. In between a bit of spoiling, of course. Meanwhile, John is on an overnight camping trip to the best fishing river in the region.

A note arrives with a terrible warning. Revenge is on the menu at the banquet. But who is the target?

People are quick to point fingers at Daphne whose sleuthing reputation precedes her. She has her own list of potential victims and even with John away, is determined to uncover the truth and keep everyone safe.

Until the only way down the mountain is blocked.

ABOUT THE AUTHOR

Phillipa lives just outside a beautiful town in country Victoria, Australia. She also lives in the many worlds of her imagination and stockpiles stories beside her laptop.

Apart from her family, Phillipa's great loves include the ocean, music, reading, the garden, and animals of all kinds.

www.phillipaclark.com

RECOMMENDED READING ORDER

The Rivers End series includes four main books (The Stationmaster's Cottage, Jasmine Sea, The Secrets of Palmerston House, The Christmas Key), plus three short books.

Taming the Wind can be read anytime. Before or after the others will still make sense.

Martha is best read after Cottage and some readers enjoyed it more after reading The Christmas Key.

There are also two spin-off series to enjoy.

The Charlotte Dean Mysteries begin shortly after The Secrets of Palmerston House. They are best read in their series order. Charlotte first appears in Jasmine Sea, effectively giving her seven books.

The Daphne Jones Mysteries are set after The Christmas

Key. These also are best read in series order. Daphne and John appear in The Stationmaster's Cottage as supporting characters.

Doctor Grok's Peculiar Shop is a series of short stories. Fantasy with a touch of magic and a lot of heart.

Last Known Contact is a stand alone crime suspense, unrelated to the other series.

Simple Words for Troubled Times is a non-fiction short book to offer comfort and happiness.

Future books include a fantasy trilogy, a new crime suspense, and more in the various series.

Thank you for reading one of my stories - I am so thrilled you took a chance on me and hope you enjoyed your time in my world.

CHARACTER NAMES ACKNOWLEDGEMENTS

Daphne's stories are a lot of fun to write and research and I'm so fortunate to have many people willing to help out. I want to do a quick shout-out to readers who were helpful with character names in this book. There were a lot of suggestions, some which will be in the next book, but for this one, my sincere thanks to Julie Gray, Marcia Ray, Carol Scotman, Patricia M Franks, and Kerrie Dean-Willcocks. I am grateful for the assistance!

Printed in Great Britain
by Amazon